MW01096957

Through The Eyes Of Tesla

Science Fiction

Fernando Fernandez

This book is especially dedicated to my mother, Mercedes, my friends Alfredo, Amelia, David, and Katherine, as well as to all my loyal readers for their unconditional support.

"The day science begins to study non-physical phenomena, it will make more progress in one decade than in all the previous centuries of its existence."
Nikola Tesla

"I don't care that they stole my idea . . I care that they don't have any of their own"
Nikola Tesla

"Of all things, I liked books best."
Nikola Tesla

They stole everything from me, including all my research findings, which took me a lifetime to complete. This is not possible. Now it's gone. Nikola is walking around; this is a nerve-breaking situation. However, I know who they are. If I go back, they will know better.

Previously, I had to come to this hotel to look for shelter. They've been kind enough to allow me to settle my things underground. They gave me space to set up my lab, as well as organized my books. What do you have there, sir? Why did you enquire? These chests are heavy. They contain the seeds of a revolution in science. How is that possible? Those papers are full of incendiary knowledge that could spark change. We will never look at the world the way we do it today. Thus, science will be transformed. I don't understand your ideas. Nevertheless, they are fascinating. You are similar to scientists today. How's that, sir? You think deeply in the hopes of understanding things around you. However, that doesn't work. You have to think lucidly. Please teach me how to do that. Clarity, my friend, comes from within. They were interrupted by the hotel manager. Are you done with Mr. Tesla's luggage? Yes, Mr. Conti. You can go back to the reception area. As Tony walked to the service elevator, he was still thinking that this conversation should continue some other time in the near future. Curiosity was killing him. He was working at the hotel to pay for his studies as well as to help his mother pay some bills. His dream was to become a renowned scientist.

Mr. Conti said, "You have our facilities at your service." Nikola smirked. Then, that man with that dull personality left.

I see them clearly. After they found Nikola's dead at the hotel, the representatives of the government's Office of Alien Property seized some of his chests. They swooped in to start looting his property. I'm impotent merely looking at them from afar. John is taking them away. There are eighty-five trunks, John. Anything else? No, there's nothing left.

The most brilliant mind in the world has come to an end. We have to discredit him more. Lunacy, craziness, or any other odd claim could be used to cover up the truth. What's the truth? That's subjective to us. John was told, "Nikola's prolific work shouldn't be analyzed; put it away from the mainstream. This is too dangerous." Are you afraid of the death ray, Mr. Graves? This war is draining our souls. This supposedly powerful particle ray must be tested by our scientists to check if it is safe for our soldiers. That would be an invaluable weapon to help us in the battle. Meanwhile, let's keep it out of the light. If our enemies got their hands on it, it would be catastrophic. Don't worry, Mr. Graves; they will be shrouded in the shadows of conspiracy or inquiries from scientists. The general population will never know what happened to these files.

After years of fielding questions, including protests requesting the files to be declassified, the bureau, which took over the operations of the former office, decided to strategically release some declassified information. Mostly harmless documents of general knowledge, speculative, or philosophical in nature. The papers that included valuable assets, ideas or methods that were modern or could be worked out to create breakthroughs, are still missing pieces of this giant puzzle left by the genius of Nikola.

John has previously worked on the development of radar systems In addition, he participated in a cohort that developed x-ray machines. He was the closest thing the government had to a scientist to deal with Nikola's research. You've got to be kidding, Alina. No, I am not, Tony. I learned a lot while he was at the hotel. Thanks to Nikola, I am now working on my dissertation. There are many scientists that could continue Nikola's work, or at least publish his books. Yes, indeed.

Different agencies are fighting over taking control of the files. Fear is everywhere. Tony was arrested for further investigation. Alina is trying to see him. Where do you have him? It was top secret. All the people who were in contact with the late scientist have been either isolated or imprisoned. They said that they want to prevent that his inventions fall in enemies hands, which is absurd. They don't have any basis for such claims. Alina visits a friend of hers. I need your help, Diana. What's wrong with you? It's my friend Tony, he was arrested. Why was he arrested? He works at the New York hotel where Nikola used to live. What a coincidence. Yes, they got along well. The authorities are afraid that he may possess some secret information that could be attractive to some foreign governments. I will check with my sources to give you a response as soon as possible. Thanks, Diana.

Alina receives a call. Who's this? A friend who wants to help you, Miss. Stop digging about the trunks. Whomever it was is not going to scare me. A few minutes later, Diana meets her. He is at the bureau. Can I see him? I will help you do that. When? What about now? Great, let's get going. Do you know anything regarding the trunks? Yes, there are sixty trunks resting somewhere in Kansas. Wait a minute, Diana. Aren't they in Belgrade? No, that was a decoy. I see. There were at least twenty five more chests, what do you think about it? Listen, Alina. They may have packed them into sixty boxes to save space. I doubt it. I'm going to seek out the truth. Be careful what you do. They are destroying whoever challenges them. It's rampant all over the country.

John has been busy writing his assessment of the knowledge that is in the boxes. I have to finish it quickly. The government is using his ideas to develop advanced technological programs.. This is crazy; wireless transmission of electrical energy. That cannot be known, that would ruin generators as well as electric companies.

Alina finally meets Tony. Are you okay? I am. However, I cannot talk about anything that involves Nikola. That's against free speech. Yes, it is. Diana comes to them. She says, "He will be released in a day or two." Alina has sought an interview with John. Forget about it! He won't talk to the press.

Alina visits some key places where she has received information of possible ongoing experiments using Nikola's ideas. This is the gigantic tower! They removed it from the hotel. I need to get closer to unravel some of the mysteries surrounding this incredible invention. When she was approaching the tower, some agents dressed in black, came to her encounter. They told her to leave, that this area was a crime scene. She replied, "There's no such crime." However, she had no other choice. Who were those enigmatic men? They must be part of some government agency. She traveled to California for clues on another groundbreaking invention that was supposedly there. She couldn't believe her eyes, on this farm, what's that? It's a unrealistic. This is something out of this world.

John was told that a reporter was closing in on him. These technologies are certainly going to build our future; don't let her get any closer. The lasting impact of what she saw at the farm is still on her mind. I need to tell somebody else. Whom should I meet? What about a scientist? Tony may help me now that he's free again.

Tony remembered one of his conversations with the genius of Nikola. He told me, "Be alone; that's the secret. That's when ideas are born." Do you remember any married men who have invented something great? No, I don't. Exactly. I am not married. I know, you are too young. Nikola was usually daydreaming, having lucid dreams, and communicating with others. However, I don't know from where. However, he had vivid interactions with non-physical entities. You are a receiver. Your brain is a recipient of the knowledge that comes from your core, your center. Where's that? It lies within you. That's the source of inspiration, the creative mind. How do I penetrate into the secrets of the core? You need to learn how to meditate. Lower your frequency to a level at which you can connect to your core, your inner authority. Then you can enquire about any questions. They will be answered with ease. It sounds simple. However, I bet it is not. Don't doubt it, my friend.

The human body is a priceless gift. From whom? From the one who loves us, from above. Do you have access to the mystery beyond human conception? Yes, that's a marvelous work of art, an indescribable beauty, everything that I feel when I invent something, the creation unfolding to success. There's no similar feeling in the world.

John has finished his report. However, he's still weighing other subjects to be included in it. The creativity of this man exceeds insanity. He decided to hand in the final draft to Mr. Graves. He was then assigned to supervise the remote viewer project in the Mojave desert. On his way to the project Nik, John took out of his pocket one small notebook with some scribbles as well as technical notes. A several hundred pages written by Nikola. He started riffling through the pages slowly. I didn't turn this in. I'm going to read it first. After a long trip, he arrived at "Project Nik."

Alina told Tony about her trip to California. They left for the desert. Upon arrival, they meet Leon, who's going to guide them as close as possible to the secret base where the project is. Where are we going, Leon? The base doesn't have a name; it is a non-existent place. "Project Nik" tests the feasibility of Nikola's concepts. The missing papers are surely there. How do you know? I have some contacts. Even though employees signed a disclaimer, it includes not talking about the non-existent place. They don't work for the government, at least not officially. They do sometimes share some information with me. We need to gain access to them. Why do you want to do that? Alina says, "This could be the best investigative work of my career." A ticket to a Pulitzer. What about you, Tony? This would boost my doctorate dissertation. You're ambitious. What about you, Leon? I'm in charge of a group that is pro-declassification of the files. They approached an electrical fence. We cannot get any closer without getting into trouble. In fact, we are in deep... A patrol swerved at the entrance, warning them that they were trespassing in a forbidden area without any other details. They told them to get on the vehicle. Then they took them to the road, where they were dropped off. If you come back, you will be imprisoned.

We simply saw was a fence, nothing else. Leon assured them, "It is an underground base." Now it makes sense. Anyway, this was a bump in the road. Don't let that disappoint you. The particle beam is in the hatching stage. However, it has been a failure because they don't fully understand how this technology works.

Nikola was ridiculed in the past; now his work is the most desirable one. It is against his intentions. They want his inventions for war: man fighting against man. The usual misunderstandings of power partnered with money are creating chaos for those who benefit from it.

John is fascinated by what he's reading. NiKola understood the nature of light, energy, vibrations, and frequencies. There's a lot of information regarding some celestial bodies, along with a wireless torpedo. The last one caught John's attention.

Nikola observes Alina and Tony. They are searching for his legacy. They mean no harm. They should get on the right track to divulge my work. Thus, make it accessible to the masses. I can manifest my thoughts in their dreams. Thus, they can continue their work successfully.

Whenever I have flashes of my past, it is nostalgic. I had four siblings. My father was an orthodox priest who instilled great values in me. Even though he pushed me to follow his steps, I didn't have his faith. Oh my! This photographic memory keeps things I wanted to delete from my mind. It seems I have to photograph my thoughts. I remember meaningless things that are supposed to be part of my short-term memory. Not in my mind. Recurrent visions were more than migraine headaches. I wanted them all to come to fruition. However, most of them went unrealized because resources were not flowing the way I wanted them to. Nobody understood my futuristic visions. They seem far-out or simply ambitious dreams. Investors were worried that my ideas were not practical enough or that they were not going to change existing practices. There were accusations that my engines were causing earthquakes. Others claimed that they were bizarre. Alien contact was not welcomed by the scientific community, although I picked up alien signals.

Hey, Tony. Are you possessed? No, I am not. What happened? You were lost for a few minutes. I was receiving some messages. From whom? Nikola himself. Are you serious? Yes, I am. Are you telling me that you are communicating with a dead man? His thoughts simply came to me. What did he tell you? We'll be able to withstand this. We will succeed.

Tony has a vivid vision. Previously, Mark came to visit Nikola. He told him, "Why don't you come live in the United States?" I haven't thought about it. As soon as Nikola arrived in New York, he started working for George. This allowed him to have his own laboratory. Thomas used electricity to power a chair for the death penalty for a convicted murderer in New York; all this to discredit George's technology, which was obtained through Nikola's patents. It ceased his royalties as well as his time with the company. That was a punch in the gut. Thus, it took their rivalry to a higher level. Prior to being adversaries, they were close friends. They would check each other's work on a daily basis, to see how their lives were going, which helped them learn about their work ethics. That was the beginning of many contributions along the way.

As Tony takes a drag, Alina looks at him. You need to look for help. I know of a great hypnotherapist. He may help you organize your ideas, at least get a better understanding. Alright, let's do it. This is mind-blowing. They meet the therapist, Dr. Angelica Wong. We often use hypnotherapy for past-life regression. In your case, we are going to reveal the secrets inside your mind. You'd better say that of the genius of Nikola manifested in me. This is not something that I don't remember. We're going to dig for something hidden in your mind. I'll assist you in connecting with the part of yourself that is communicating with a paranormal being. Simply some facts about that link, to decide whether it is a delirium or a real connection to Nikola's mind. We are going back to the moment in which you started experiencing these memory implants. Alina stays behind. She asks the therapist, "Is he suffering from some mental issues?" I need to continue the therapy to identify his condition.

These awe-inspiring inventions would be appreciated by future generations. My brilliant, somehow confused life. I shared my insomnia with my beloved creatures, the pigeons at the park. I didn't have a mind for business. People were amused by my inventions. However, they were puzzled by me. They couldn't understand how I would prefer being alone than sharing with others. Solitude, along with silence, brought me peace of mind. That was, to my imagination, the spark that triggered most of my creations. Recognition or wealth were never my motives.

Tony is back for the second session of therapy. Let's begin with relaxation. A paused, soft voice, slowly conducting me through the process. Next, we're going to start with visualization. The therapist asked me some open-ended questions. I talk about what I recalled, what I saw. Please continue with whatever comes to your mind regarding that particular moment. I still feel what I did that day. Now I am aware of what happened. We're consciously examining the memories retrieved. Dr. Wong is analyzing the facts by reexamining the recording of the session. You have to put it in perspective. Why did you retrieve that memory now? What does it mean? You need to fully understand why it is essential to you. You can answer those questions later or in the next session. How do you feel, Tony? I'm a little lightheaded. However, I'm okay. What did you learn? I learned a lot. He wanted me to continue his legacy.

Alina thinks that this is controversial. She doesn't buy it that fast. What if she was leading you to believe what she expected you to think? You mean, some kind of directed memory implant? Sort of. You're skeptical, Alina. She didn't create any fake memories. There are vivid images in my mind. I sensed a nervous breakdown that he suffered after dropping out of school due to a lack of money for the tuition. I additionally recall him walking through the park with a friend. He was using a malacca stick. I can see the pigeons. Then he started reciting poetry. He drew something on the dirt floor with the stick. What was that? It was a magnetic engine. Induction? That was the principle behind that technology. Wow, that's awesome. Why did you stop talking? He had a vision back then. What was that? Aliens, aliens from Orion, aliens, aliens, aliens, aliens, aliens, aliens. Are you sure? Yes, I am. I can see them. They are right in front of my eyes. Watch out, Tony! What? Look at the sky. As they were walking out of the therapist's office, the sky above had a spaceship hovering. They panicked!
Nikola is at peace with his mind as well as his soul. Tony remembers the things I taught him. I hope he

15

takes action. That's what all this is about, to transform the world.

We should forget about all this. No way, Alina. I will get to the bottom of this. You may get into trouble with the authorities. Why is that? They may think that you are either a time traveler or an alien. You know too many details regarding Nikola. You may be right.

Nikola arrived in New York for the first time, with merely four cents and a recommendation letter from Charles. Thomas hired him, with some reserve. He neither liked his humor nor his business-oriented practice. That made Nikola quit soon. The competition between them will turn into an unprecedented rivalry due to patents, inventions. Although it was mostly caused by Thomas' greed.

A job digging ditches would at least bring food to the table. Not long after that, Western Bank got word of mouth regarding Nikola's engine. They were willing to invest in its invention. I didn't try to improve my first design; it went straight from the board to the manufacturing. My vision was made real, exactly what I saw in my dreams. This is a deja vu. A picture of my thoughts expressed in reality. How gratifying it was. A war of currents was ignited.

Nikola made a huge mistake. George, his previous employer, begged him to set him free from paying the royalties for the engine he had previously developed. Since George never tried to swindle him, Nikola decided to tear up the contract. He then said goodbye to his royalties. That avoided George's company going bankrupt, which eventually sealed his successful fate. What could have meant billions in royalties for Nikola or made him the richest man in the world, turned out to be a non-profit invention.

After some failures, Nikola told himself, "My priority is to look for a sponsor for my projects." I came across J.P. This partnership was beneficial for both parties. While J.P. had a lot of money, he wanted to invest in opportunities that came up at the moment. On the other hand, Nikola was eager to develop his projects. I began building communications networks with a giant tower. I soon ran out of funds. By then J.P. balked at Tesla's white elephant. Although they were magnificent ideas, which required excessive amounts of money, their results were not understood by many.

At the same time, Guglielmo was working with radio waves. Telegraphy made him a celebrity. Later in life, while studying the transmission of wireless signals, including waves, more accurately, he helped develop microwave technology. He spent many years trying to detect outer space signals. He contacted some advanced civilization. That could have been his lucky break. His friend Nikola was exploring frequencies as well as waves too. They usually compared notes and partnered for some secret projects. A common trait, they become detached at the end of their lives, contacting alien entities. Nikola withdrew from this unfriendly, voracious world. Doctors said, "He was suffering from an obsessive-compulsive disorder." However, this highly functional genius thought that they were wrong. He detached from the world to pursue his dreams, contacting alien civilizations on a larger scale. His odd behavior, cleanliness, as well as a fixation on the numbers 3, 6, and 9 were considered signs of' madness. There's a thin line between madness and genius. After shaking hands, he used to wash right away to avoid germs or any bacteria. As well as possible contagious viruses or diseases. He preferred everything divisible by 3, such as hotel rooms with the number 36. He used 18 napkins during meals. He would count his steps wherever he went. My senses are enhanced now. I have an acute sense of hearing as well as an extraordinary sight. Furthermore, that has a downsize. That's causing me an abnormal sensitivity to some sounds that are not perceived by humans. The aversion to earrings is due to that slight movement of a pearl rubbing against the metal. I have a privileged hearing that my ears can catch that sound. That's annoying to me. Light is another problem. It is not photophobia; it is simply that I see other things ranging outside of the spectrum we usually see. It hurts my optical nerves. Another weird story I told my friend Guglielmo: a white pigeon would come to my hotel window. I loved that bird more than any human. Our communication was strong. One day, the pigeon came to me to tell me that she was dying. I could see two beams of light coming from her eyes, more intense than anything I had seen before. Not even the most powerful lamp I had in my laboratory could reproduce such luminosity. That powerful, dazzling light from above was surely a signal that her end was near. Ever since that moment, I knew I had to retire. However, I kept a low profile to continue working secretly in the hotel's basement, which communicated with the old city subway system. This underground maze served my purpose.

My experiments, from time to time, caused lights to flicker all over the city. The high demand for electricity caused a total blackout a couple of times. Nevertheless, nobody could link them to me or my tower. How naive they were. I was under their buildings, in their city. My projects were inconclusive. I was in debt, although George continued paying for my hotel room. I guess it was a gesture of gratitude for all the money my invention brought to him as well as for his company.

Some foreign governments tried unsuccessfully to develop the death beam. They had the design. However, they lack the acumen to understand Nikola's mind, what materials to use or how to assemble the device.

Tony is back at Dr. Wong's office. This time, Alina couldn't make it. She had to report on a special event the president was attending. Dr. Wong said, "You are neither his reincarnation nor possessed." What's going on in my mind? That's why you are here. We're going to find out about it. You have his memories embedded in your long-term memory. It is something unseen in science. I have reached out to my faculty colleagues to see if they can recall any similar cases in the past. You and your mentor share a common trait. What's that, Doc? You have a high IQ. You may be a savant. What? Yes, you demonstrate some abilities far in excess of the average person; unusual skills that normal people don't possess, such as rapid calculation, mind-mapping, abstract thinking, hypersensitivity to sounds or light, and most importantly, memory. Do you have an eidetic memory? A what? A photographic memory? Yes, I can remember images easily. We are going to run some tests to discard some possible options, such as autism, brain injury, mental disorders, tumors... Wait a minute! Is this dangerous? We can't tell until we have the results. Don't jump to conclusions that fast. Is that condition common? No, it isn't. One in a million people is a savant. I remember that Nikola had an exceptional memory, an advanced memory that was his superpower. What was his weakness? His social interaction was poor. Don't get me wrong. He was eloquent, as well as persuasive. He didn't love people. Did he suffer from Asperger's syndrome? No, Tony. Every person has a different diagnosis. What about my case? It may be possible. Some types of functional autism are distinguished by repetitive patterns of behavior, or limited interests combined with a lack of social interaction. Nevertheless, Nikola had excellent communication skills. He would perform above average in most skills. He was a prodigy. This is not a diagnosis at all; it should be a broader spectrum disorder. Furthermore, we need to focus on your case right now.

The results of the analysis came out today. Dr. Wong is reading them. She called Tony to ask him to join her and her colleagues at the university. Upon arrival, Tony greets them. I am not going to beat around the bush. Let's go straight to the point. You are not autistic. However, you have a central nervous system injury. It appears to have undergone surgery. I have never had any surgery at all. This is weird. That's exactly what I thought. Here's Dr. Slaton. He is a neurosurgeon. He's going to run some MRIs to verify the results. Alright.

Alina is interviewing the president. She asks, "Are you going to recognize the genius of the late Nikola?" The question was not surprising. However, it disgusted the authorities. She had to return to work with no answer. What am I going to tell my boss? Well, it was not my fault. He didn't answer the question of this young rebel.

In some cases, a savant could be induced by trauma. Is that his case? I'm not sure, Angelica. What do you think? To be honest, I didn't find any scars on his skin or any sutures on his bones that indicated that there was a fracture or an intervention. If that happened, there should be some fibrous joint that scarcely occurs in the skull. Could it have been an untreated injury? Not of such magnitude. I doubt it. A similar case has never been seen before. It is unlikely to happen. If you got such an injury, it would mean instant death. Wow, that's exceeding the rarity level. It's getting spooky.

Alina is concerned about Tony. She didn't have her support in the last week, since she has been busy. She will join him along with Dr. Wong's team tomorrow. When the morning comes, she gets ready for her appointment at Dr. Wong's office. She rushes to arrive on time. Dr. Wong explains to Alina that the most probable issue is a social pragmatic disorder, which somehow overlaps symptoms with Asperger's. Does Tony seem awkward in social situations? Not that I have noticed. Does he know what to say when he talks to strangers? He may be shy. However, he's talkative when he gets to know you. What about body language and mannerisms? Listen, Doc. He's not such a freak. Does he cross his arms and scowl? No, that's not him. Something happened to Tony after meeting the scientist. He's changed.

Tony was thinking about some of these questions. Nikola showed few emotions; that was his way. He didn't laugh at jokes, not that he didn't understand them. He disliked vulgarity, gross or distasteful things. He, indeed, talked to himself most of the time. Nevertheless, he was an eccentric scientist, a mastermind who disliked loud people.

Tony is struck by blinding flashes. He is having a vision. The light envelops my mind, which fills my brain with things I've never seen; brilliant ideas, shimmering lights. This is the solution to a problem I've been pondering. An idea for a modern invention is born. My head is imploding. Is this inspiration? No, this is an external pressure. This is an ordeal!

Alina notices that Tony has changed. Now he's reading voraciously. What are you reading?Huckleberry Finn, then Tom Sawyer,... You have never read any of his books, have you? No, I haven't. Why the sudden interest in his books? I received a telepathic message from him saying that I had to read Mark's books. This is such a beneficial therapy for me. Therapy for what? It's intended to appease my inner demons. Another thing I noticed is your photographic memory. What's wrong with it? It has evolved into an eidetic memory. You can recall complete diagrams, blue prints, or your own thoughts as pictures or mini-movies. That's true. I don't even have to draw them. His acumen is coming to you. You are the chosen one. You know that brilliance comes with eccentricity, which indicates fears that may engulf you. I must not surrender to his fears or phobias. How are you going to choose what to keep or what to let go? I don't want to suffer from OCD in my life, any obsessive rituals, or superstitions.

He never married since he felt he could never be worthy enough for a woman. He believed that romantic life and love, along with intimacy would interfere with his scientific research. What about you, Tony? I think I love you, Alina. You're a sweetheart. I think I should devote my life to science, though. Alina has been recording his conversations with Tony. She will share them with Dr. Wong.

This is going to be the final therapy session. I won't return to them. There's much I have to do. Dr. Wong starts talking to him. My colleagues couldn't make it today. That's alright. Let's start with some questions. How many languages do you speak? I speak eight languages fluently. Did you learn any of those recently? Yes, indeed. I could barely speak one language before I was gifted. Do you have any recurring dreams? Not exactly. However, I usually find myself daydreaming or experiencing disgusting visions of animal electrocutions. Do you see who is performing these killings? Thomas. Do you have any feelings about it? Yes, sadness, disappointment, as well as anger.

A spacecraft is stealthy above the lab. Lights bathe the area. Tony is covered by light, as if he's in a bubble of light. Dr. Wong is perplexed, while

Alina is more concerned about his mental health. Look at the evidence. It's happening now. Tony is not crazy. I know he is not. However, this is way too much. The local authorities have sent some airplanes to approach the alien spacecraft. Unexpectedly, some figures emerged from a beam. Nikola is accompanied by two thin beings. Tony walks peacefully to meet them. They were off to the stars in the blink of an eye. Our pilots couldn't do anything. They were trying to follow the aliens. However, they couldn't match such speed. A triangular spacecraft that is absolutely out of this world. One of the pilots reported, "They disappeared in front of our eyes. There was a disturbance in mid-air, sort of a portal." They went through a fold in a ply of space-time, straight to a distant part of the universe. Alina read the report. Her reaction was that they time traveled, or flew away to a faraway land unknown to us. Nikola is still alive there. Tony is gone. What's next? I don't know.

John is talking to Mr. Graves. There was a design for a similar spacecraft among his papers. Can we reverse engineer it? If there's somebody that can do that, it's Thomas. Gather whoever you need to accomplish this task. Previous works have been woefully incomplete or plain wrong due to the lack of understanding of alien technology.

This is uncharted territory. Tony is in outer space. Face to-face with Nikola. Are you the real deal? What do you think? You must be a clone. Otherwise, you are over one hundreds sixty years old. What if it is possible in this part of the cosmos? Do you think that is possible? We have achieved many things, including immortality. I don't believe you are the same old person that I met long ago. Why did you enquire then? I guess it is human nature. Do you need reassurance? No, not this time. Why did you bring me here? You have a mission to accomplish. What is that? You have to tell your people about a curse that awaits you in the near future. What's that? Easy, young man. When the time comes, we'll let you know. Why me? You are the chosen one. How did you choose me? Have you ever heard of the collective consciousness of the cosmos? Sort of. Our souls are part of the flow of consciousness that surrounds the universe.

The news spread all over. It couldn't be hidden anymore. We are too vulnerable. What's beyond the universe? Another universe. These aliens seem powerful. Their flight was effortless. They are using quantum gravity through a white hole. They mastered the use of multiple dimensions. What's more, they've traveled through the multiverse. Do you remember your parents? You know, inventing the future is in my veins. My bloodline was built on inventions. My mother was an inventor who created advanced tools even though she was living in a remote area far away from civilization. Moreover, my father contributed to my creativity. My life has changed ever since I came across this advanced civilization.

The convergence of different countries with different interests to create a plan to face a possible alien invasion is absolutely unifying. He's intrepid enough to go to that length to follow in the footsteps of the trailblazing Nikola. The legendary man has returned. How is that possible? The mad scientist definitely found some help. From whom? He must have been helped by some beings of an advanced civilization.

Dr. Wong's office, along with her colleagues, is being visited by John. He raided the lab, looking for any evidence of their work. This is illegal. How come? This has never happened before, professors. His men collected all their papers. They left as quickly as they got here. Why did they do that? They are terrified of the uproar that the alien threat is posing over the world. They want to keep this secret. While people are still in the dark, they are in control. They will go after Tony. They cannot do that because he was abducted by aliens right in front of my eyes. Do you have any evidence? Everybody who was around campus yesterday witnessed their presence. We missed it. Yes, you did. What about Alina? Have you referred to her in any of your writings? No, I haven't. Nevertheless, I'm afraid that her voice is in some of the recordings. We have to warn her of what's coming. She's a reporter. Therefore, she must be aware of what's going on. Anyway, I will call her.

Dr. Wong contacted Alina. They told her what had happened at the lab. Be safe. I will try. Alina walks out of his apartment building, across the street. However, she was intercepted by two men dressed in black. Come with me. She had no choice. She climbed into a black SUV, where John was waiting for her. I was told that you were looking for me. Yes, I was. Here I am. What can I do for you, reporter? I wanted to interview you regarding the missing papers of the late Nikola. Why are you interested in the mad scientist trunks? Not the trunks, the contents. They contain valuable information that could change the future. That's top secret. You know that confidential information is not revealed to the general public. I know all that. Why did you disclose some selected papers? You are smarter than that, Ms. A decoy? Let's call it simply a distraction during agitated times. The turmoil surrounding Nikola's reappearance is upsetting authorities. Although, your friend joining him in an endeavor to explore an unknown world is fascinating to the public. Am I your prisoner? No, you are not. Why are you talking to me? I am saving you time and effort. I am answering all of your questions. What exactly do you want from me, John? Where's Tony? I don't know. He may be in outer space with Nikola in conjunction with the aliens. How am I supposed to know that? Well, you are close. Yes, we are. What do you know about what happened to your friend? That's what Dr. Wong had been trying to find out about before the abduction. However, it seems that you scared her and her team. Have you thought that the abduction case was staged? Not at all. How come? Somebody may have disguised a plane. Therefore, all this madness was staged. You are an expert at covering up for the government. Nevertheless, you forgot, I guess intentionally, some vital details. Which ones? The speed and the maneuverability of the spacecraft are beyond question, not from this world. You may have a point, young lady. What about Nikola? I don't have the faintest idea, sir. Do you think that he could be a time traveler? Alina replied, "You don't belong in these modern times, John." You are clever, reporter. Your friend Tony is a smart guy. Is he another time traveler? What? This is too much. Answer my question. I'm almost sure that all of you are time travelers. John didn't deny it. He ordered his team to release her.

You told me that you are part of the collective consciousness of the cosmos. Are aliens too? Yes, we are all one. How did you become Nikola? Even though we have a large genetic bank, I was not created. I am myself. Do you have my genes? That's one of the reasons you were brought here. If you are neither a clone nor created, what else are you? I am Nikola. My consciousness was uploaded to the cosmos. All my memories were digitized. However, they will always be part of me. What do you know about me? I know everything. Are you dead? I am dead. However, alive in some another dimension. I am more than a soul in the realm of consciousness.

There's more to the cosmos than what we get to see. Not even our most advanced telescopes can show us a hint of its vastness. There are limits regarding your senses even current technology, Tony. Show me the way, master of light. What if we traveled all the way straight at the speed of light, or even faster? Do you want to know where you will end up at some point along the way? Yes, I'm curious about the frontier between universes. You won't hit a wall, although there are some walls on the outskirts of galaxies. What kind of walls? They are basically hot plasma. Are there any boundaries to the universe? If we were in a linear, unidimensional universe, you'd surely hit a wall or fall. However, it turns out that space-time curves creating portals that take you to other dimensions or universes in the multiverse. That goes into outright lunacy, simply madness. How much, in addition to the observable universe, exists? It is a gargantuan number. We can barely see an infinitesimally small percentage of the whole cosmos. You are making my brain hurt. Particles in quantum fields create universes, then they expire. Thus, other incipient ones take their places in a cycle that repeats itself. Who was our parent universe? That requires time travel to the big bang moment. Can we do that? Sure, everything is possible in this dimension. What about human life? It didn't originate on Earth. Are you talking about panspermia? Sort of. If you remember, our ancestors were such primitive creatures, then unexpectedly they turned into Homo sapiens with no link between them. How did it happen? Our DNA was probably enhanced. They were space travelers, the survivors of an almost extinct advanced civilization. What caused their collapse? Technology? No, not at all. Ambition, for the most part, along with disputes with other worlds.

Can our government track us or find us here? They don't have such technology yet. They must be having a bad time justifying their actions, why they were weak enough that they couldn't prevent your abduction from happening.

They may think that we are dead. Aren't you? That's relative. There are many dead universes, including voids. What's more there you may find inter-dimensional beings. We live in a pokey corner of a universe, which is an anomaly with plenty of life. When are we going back to our planet? You are, not me. I'm part of the collective consciousness of the cosmos now.

Alina is overwhelmed by all the recent unfortunate events. With a bit of savviness, you can do a few things, such as keeping a low profile, while actively searching for Tony's time machine. I feel that he is going to be back soon. Tony clearly possesses a prowess for science. That mental ability to read people's minds, I guess Nikola passed it on to him.

My consciousness was shared with you. That's why I feel this way. What is that? If I were you. Listen, you are me. I exist in many realms. Although I can travel anywhere, not everybody can see me.

Mr. Graves is watching the surveillance videos from some news channels' footage regarding the alien incident. He calls a friend. I need your help with some videos. What do you need, Mr. Graves? Check if this is authentic. I think there's something fishy about this alien abduction. Something doesn't fit. Okay, I will be back to you in a few days. Not at all. I don't have that much time. I want a report by tomorrow. I'll do my best, sir. Experts weigh in on the authenticity of these images. The forthcoming report will clarify what happened.

Mr. Graves is reading the report. The videos show an incident that is unusual. For more than five minutes, some jets were tailgating an UFO, with no other spacecraft in sight, which is highly suspicious, since they are usually accompanied by others. Although videos help a lot, eyewitness accounts are first-hand testimony. Their version of this odd sighting found their way into the public view through the news. In addition, social media made it viral. They are ultimately spurring the demand that the government clarify this encounter. Emergency protocols were activated to deny it. They even tried to discredit what had happened in plain sight. National security is a must. We can't acknowledge such an attack since it may indicate that we are vulnerable to these beings. Mr. Graves is assessing the report. I have to read between the lines. These guys are not disclosing the most essential parts of the report. Mr. Graves called John to get the complete report. He sent his people to the unit to drag the technician with the report. I need that information urgently. I understood.

Your mission is to prevent the world being destroyed by ambitious politicians or greedy businessmen. I will do as you say, Nikola. Do I have to time travel? Whatever it is, you don't have to worry at all. This has been a paranormal experience. Am I dead? We are all alive. Even though some people say that we are both at the same time. Somewhere in the multiverse, you are alive. While in another dimension, you may be dead. What am I taking with me? You are taking with you all my knowledge. My consciousness will guide you too. You will see through my eyes, Tony. Isn't it the other way around? No, my friend. I am going to be your guide from now on.

Meanwhile, all the oddities have extensively garnered the attention of the public. What's more, Alina is investigating what the government knows about the incident. Strangeness through it all. A sizeable mass of UFO believers gathers in front of Congress demanding the declassification of information regarding aliens. Alina asks Diana, "Why are they cautious about this topic?" It's a matter of national security. Are we defenseless when these beings are slipping through our skies? Don't say that again. This reinvigorated Alina's investigation. Moreover, there are entrenched beliefs. There are government efforts to cover them up. All these can lead to dazzling speculation or even wrong assumptions. The disclosure of information has been a mere formality, without revealing any vital information. Censors are publicly backing up the disclosure. However, privately, they are pushing to hold up the most valuable information.

Mr. Graves received John's report. I had to... Please save the details. I hope you didn't leave any evidence behind. No, I didn't. Any incidents involving the high levels of government should be avoided. When he starts reading it, he notices some flaws in our security. What defenses? They are useless. This is why they forbade this report. It was a hologram! A mere projection. It was staged by the aliens. How did they abduct Tony? There was a beam. From where? It came from nowhere, then vanished. We looked like a bunch of dummies. The report's firmest conclusion is that their surprising maneuvers are the result of advanced technology. Celestial phenomena? Who the heck wrote this report? My source was forced to produce this piece of inept narrative.

Alina contacted a clandestine organization that has been promoting the protests, whether challenging the government or promoting a secret agenda. They agreed to meet her soon. I have to hurry to the meeting point. That must be them. Young lady, why do you want to meet us? Although the task force's unclassified assessment is public, I think there's something more to this incident. You are right. Our sources indicated that this was a set up for your friend. Who did it? Aliens, of course. What sources? I can't reveal them. You can at least be more specific. Alright. Some senior officials familiar with the alien agenda told us that the assessment came up short intentionally. Why is that? They are covering up evidence of any putative visitation of alien beings. We have information deemed unsuitable for public release, which suggests that the government is hiding the truth. As a reporter, I know that the media has lavished too much attention on sensational, untrue claims, mostly conspiracy theories. A flurry of misleading efforts that the government has launched to distract or confuse the public won't be enough to prevent the truth from being revealed. What was the supposed leak? There was no spacecraft. How come? They staged everything. Who? The aliens did. Imagine that I accepted what you said. What's the purpose? They don't need a spacecraft to travel. They can do this at will. How? We don't know that yet. You are speculating. No, we are not. There's even more. What we saw coincided with what was caught on video; it is nothing more than a hologram. A projection? Yes, exactly that. Your friend was teleported using a beam. That's what you think happened. Not simply us, there are more people that back us up on this. We have a copy of John's report. That's great. You asked too many questions. You have to learn to listen, then enquire. Sorry, I've been under a lot of pressure.

Tony is almost ready to go back to Earth. Our consciousness is intertwined with theirs. Even though you are still alive, you belong to us. To whom? The consciousness. I'll guide you all the way. You will see through my eyes with my mindset, acumen, and patience to deal with inconvenient situations.

Mr. Graves is trying to decode a piece of the report that was censored to avoid public access. They took the time to cover these lines. Is there any procedure to make it visible? You don't have to reinvent the wheel. Let's call for help. Mr. Graves contacted one of his informers to get the entire paragraph without any censorship.

The general public is unaware of the exotic materials the government is in possession of. This includes alien DNA. What may be the endgame here? Somebody else has to answer that question. The authorities have drafted the analysis of these out-of-this-world materials for their own advantage.

A stronghold for the general belief that aliens are among us. Is that true? Mr. Graves listens carefully to his informant. Tell me the transcription of the specific paragraph I asked you to decode. It literally reads, "They are spirits that float into space. They go wherever they want without a spacecraft. They mean no threat to us, so far. We recommend total annihilation of the invaders." That's it? No, sir. They mentioned, "We have no means to destroy them. If Tony, the abducted human, is returned, we must question him to get some answers." Thanks.

John had failed before. This is the time to ensure that everything runs smoothly. The spaceship is going to be tested in a couple of days. I will let Mr. Graves know about the development. They are managing some dangerous goods. They are wearing some special gear to protect themselves from radiation. They may even find some possible biological pathogens. They have a crystal box containing some exotic alien material. It is moving, it is alive. What's that thing? It is similar to jellyfish. However, it is mutating into something else. This is hushed up, a top secret project. They won't acknowledge the use of this alien material in the design of this biological spacecraft. This may become a tense moment in international relations. Not even diplomacy could solve the dispute that will result over who has the right to the alien technology.

Alina is sure that they won't come clean; they won't admit what they are doing either. This is a ridiculously elaborate plan. How far across the government is the truth hidden? I can answer that. Tony! Yes, my dear. You're back. Yes, I am. Tell me, what happened? To make a long story short, since I met Nikola, we're one. I see through his eyes. Furthermore, I possess his knowledge. How is that possible? Everything is possible in the universe. The limitations come from our own minds as well as from restrictions that authorities set to keep us in the dark. What are you going to do? I'm going to get my trunks back; all my research is in them.

Mr. Graves tells the crew, "This is an astonishing feat. It is impressive how you reverse engineered this spacecraft. The project got going, ultimately integrating exotic biological material." This is an outstanding accomplishment. We started with lofty aims. However, we ended up establishing a precedent for future space exploration. I congratulate all of you for all your efforts to flawlessly accomplish the assembly of this structure. There was cheering and applause from the engineers and technicians working on the project. The most nerve-wracking part has been done successfully. The completion of this challenging procedure brought relief, along with joy, to the crew. This spacecraft is a seamless breakthrough. You perfectly executed the deployment of the different parts. The test of the spacecraft went well. Can we keep going with the rest? We still have a lot of work to do. We have to achieve the same level of perfection regarding the modules on board, including the one for warp speed.

Against all odds, Tony arrived yesterday safely on Earth. As soon as he got to his place, he met Alina. Alina told him that he looked different. How come? Yes, your eyes have that deep, inquisitive look. Don't worry, I am still the same old person that you know. As he walks by, Alina notices that his body is changing. You are turning into Nikola. I am him already. His magnificent mind was not fully appreciated. Since he was ahead of his time, none of his designs or inventions were valued. That man was born in the wrong era. He received lots of insults and humiliation. What are you going to do, Tony? I am going to get my trunks back. I need my research papers. I have no time to waste. They want to construct all my inventions. They are working on some of them. My first task is to stop them, then recover my inventions. They have evil purposes. Do you know where they are, Alina? Not at all. However, I know who can help us find them. That sounds great.

People should be more open to modern theories now, especially after the alien visitations. We're trying to achieve the impossible: get inside Nikola's head to decode his creations. You'll surely find practical uses for all of them. John approaches Mr. Graves. He handed in a manuscript. Where did you get it? I... Don't tell me, you've kept it all this time. I was reading it to analyze its potential. Did you find anything attractive to us? It is quite amusing. It has different ways of harnessing energy on Earth and in the sun. A group of men dressed in black entered the project's office. What are you doing here? We came for the manuscript. Do you know this is a secret project? You are not supposed to disrupt our peace this way. We know who you are and what you are doing. We don't care anything about that. All we want is the document. If we need to take it, we'll do it. They had merely one choice, to surrender the document to these gentlemen.

Who do you think they work for? They seem to be a special unit assigned by the president herself to prevent any leaks of incendiary material of alien origin. Do you have any copies? Of course, I do. I saved the document, I have it on my laptop. Here you are.

Mr. Graves made some calls. After a while, he received an invitation to meet the president. It was such a short-notice invitation, that he had to rush to get to his appointment on time. What is going to happen to me? I don't know. What about the project? I don't know either. Right now everything is in jeopardy. He got to his destination. Later he was conducted to a meeting room, where there were some advisors. He greeted them all. However, he had to wait patiently for the president's arrival. She didn't make them wait long. Gentlemen, let's get into business. Ma'am President. What do you have in mind for keeping top-secret documents, Mr. Graves? I didn't mean to keep them; I was going to turn them in. I'd received them when those men took us by surprise. You ought to improve the security of the project. Yes, ma'am. Do you have anything else to tell me? Yes, Nikola had anti-gravity technology. You see, you keep on hiding information. We've retrieved the energy-harnessing device. Now you've come up with recent findings. Have a productive talk with the scientists that will work on that project. See you later, guys.

What exactly are we talking about? We're going to discuss his dynamic theory of gravity in detail. That would have a significant impact on modern life. His great mind was finally understood. It surely was frustrating since people called him a magician, among some other names. We must start right now. Bring us all the documents. I will do that.

Alina is taking Tony to talk to Diana. On their way, Tony says, "I began to believe in old alchemical mysticism." You are talking similarly to him. Sorry, I can't help it. All his magical devices could exist for the sake of a better world. That's dangerous; it could change the landscape of the world. Leaders of powerful nations will be against your ideas. They won't have any other choice. As soon as Diana met them, she rushed them to tell her what the matter was since she sensed that she was being followed by members of another government agency. Where are the trunks? That's what you are after. Yes, we want to save them from those monsters. They are in a supposedly abandoned base. Where is that? I can give you the location later. I've got to go. Do the same for your own safety. She disappeared in the dark of the night. What was all that? Let's move. Don't wait until somebody comes after us.

Diana sent Alina a picture of an observatory in the desert. Where's that? It's in Arizona. There we go. The base is not in the observatory. Where do you think it is? She's going to send another clue. We'll wait over there. Alright, I understand. This frenetic behavior is confusing Alina. What happened to him while he was in outer space? Was he transformed? I won't ask him about it. It may change the trust he has in me. I know what you are thinking. Did you read my mind? I can do many things. Nevertheless, rest assured that nothing else happened to me.

The second task is to fully deploy wireless technologies around the Earth. That will turn our planet into an enormous brain. It will have light rings around the equator, similar to those of Saturn. Telepathy and telekinesis will be part of our daily lives, no matter where we are. Intuition will be another enhanced sense. I constantly hear a voice coming from everywhere, in all directions, that tells me what to do. It's a chant, a sad lament at times, or even a prayer. Aren't you sure what it is? It's a mixture of all of them. When I returned to my senses, I realized that these were instructions rather than commands. I strongly believe this voice comes from within. It is my core. Your own consciousness? It's our shared consciousness. I get confused from time to time. I didn't confide this to anyone. Not even to my doctor, since I've lost my trust in him. I could feel people's suffering. From my mother, I sense sadness, pain, and despair. What about now, Tony? Yes, I perceive some. It is increasing by the hour. Do you hear the voice when you are sleeping? Yes, I do. Sometimes even when I am wide awake. I know it sounds crazy. However, I haven't lost my sanity yet.

Alina and Tony drove to a waterfall. What are we going to do there, Tony? Trust me, I need to do this. He dropped off the car, then started shouting at the voice. Can you hear it? No, I can't. Alina was worried about him. There were some workers. He told them, "Prepare the turbines. Wait for my call tomorrow." Are you coming back tomorrow? I don't know, I guess I will. They will wait for my call.

He mumbled that governments are basically the same here as back home. One man cannot change the world on his own. I need the government to back up my work. Why did you say all that back there? This voice is still annoying me. However, it is somehow linked to you, Tony. Why don't you try to understand who is talking to you? Why? You're right.

Tony entered Congress. Later, he interrupted the session. He asked for a couple of minutes to talk to the congressmen. He told them, "I was returned from alien soil. I am Nikola's consciousness." Everybody was perplexed, including Alina. What can we do for you, sir? I want my trunks back. They listened to him. He added, "The turbines at Niagara Falls were turned on. They are ten fold more powerful." They will verify that. He left before the security came to remove him from the building. Poor guy, he lost his mental health after the abduction. One congressman said, "He is the genius of the man." What do you mean? He achieved greatness, similarly to the man who invented a whole different world. We may be missing something big here. If we leave something completely unrecognized, future generations will.

Tony says, "I don't care about what they think; they are a bunch of bureaucrats." The voice is speaking to me again. It is some formula that is not within the grasp of my understanding. I have failed. Congress ignored my petition. I don't want to clarify this formula. It must be related to... Hurry, Tony. They are coming after us. My lab is burning. No, Tony, that's merely your imagination. It's a vision, a vivid memory from Nikola. Get rid of it until we get to a safe haven. I saw Thomas first. Then I saw John. They burned it! What? The lab has the formulas written on its walls.

Mr. Graves is adamant that Tony must be questioned regarding recent projects.

Nikola had become such an indifferent person that he couldn't stand himself. I may have felt sad before. Nevertheless, this time is a terrible sorrow. My discoveries are not mine anymore. They are using my designs, blueprints, and the materials I chose. How dare they do that? They are cynics. In the past, humankind was not ready for my inventions. Now, they are eager to try everything I have done. One thing is that they are not giving the credit that Nikola deserves. They have a plan to accomplish them. He is still a part of us. His life is not over for greatness. He's a pure consciousness resting upon us. I won't avoid these terms; I have to do whatever it takes to get things done as the late Nikola instructed.

Mr. Graves knew more about this than I did. Although he's not a scientist, he manages everything with aplomb. John is walking down the hall on his way to a congressional session. All these years spent working in science in government, however, I still don't know him. Experience is not enough to deal with such a wolf. This is for great deeds.

In Earth's inner core, there are joy, love, and peace vibrations. These are three vibrations. They are the expressions of life on Earth, such as the flowers that bloom, the fruit and food harvested by agriculture, the animals that breed, and humans. Listen, Alina. This energy influences people. The beauty is in the symmetry of nature as well as in the sun's rays that nourish us.

Strange reports are circulating on Earth. However, eyewitnesses are not coming forward to give their accounts. They are unable to express what they have witnessed with mere words. Over the last few days, many unidentified aerial phenomena have been reported along with mysterious anomalies such as auroras, bursts of electricity, electromagnetic waves, and many lights of bright colors. They were disguised as meteorites. However, they move unnaturally; they could fly or change direction in unimagined ways. Authorities were quick to discredit the testimonies. They attributed the phenomena to ball lightning, meteorites, and other natural events. Although this activity is on the rise, they don't pretend to admit it. Mr. Graves is aware of what is going on. They are coming for the spacecraft. However, it is too late. Our scientists have engineered some of his inventions. Moreover, they have unraveled some of the secrets of the universe.

Tony told Alina, "It's time." For what? It's time to decipher the signals coming from outer space. Those anomalies are giving us a hint as to which way we should go. I have to renew contact with aliens. Light and energy are all around us. He started listening for hours, days, weeks, and even months. Alina was concerned that Tony may have lost his sanity. He thinks he's Nikola. He's detached from the world. Tony shouted, "I know what they are telling us." Did you translate their message? I don't need to do that. I see the world through Nikola's eyes. If you did that, it would be a groundbreaking discovery. Tony started singing hyms to electromagnetic energy. There's a second message. What is it? It is: "We're hunters of light. Earth is our next target." That's horrific. It is indeed. Are there any other messages? Yes, I am trying to understand them. "We caught light with our net from the depths of celestial bodies." What do they mean by net? It may be some sort of light trap. Not at all. It's an extraction tool to harness energy from multiple sources. I see it clearly now. It's a cannon-like device that absorbs light from stars and the cores of planets. It sends waves that create earthquakes.

There are other fragments of different messages. They want to be called the supreme, "Five races will prey on you in the temple of the future." It's a curse, Tony. It is undoubtedly not a blessing. "Nikola had taught a great secret: that Empedocles elements can be watered with the life forces of the ether." What are the Empedocles' elements? Empedocles was a Greek philosopher who believed that matter was formed of four elements: earth, fire, water, and air. What are the life forces of the ether? These are the forces that create matter. They make its environment appear as a whole. The four ethers are: warmth, light, sound, and magnetism. These four forces are the formative forces that constitute the physical world. Is there any other world besides the physical one? Yes, indeed. For instance, the spiritual world. These forces manifest in different ways. For instance, warmth manifests as fire, heat,... We are detecting more messages. These are waves. Let's reduce the white noise to receive them clearly.

The life force is a mystery to us. It has different names. Chi, Prana, and the ether element are similar. However, they have slightly different characteristics. The message is clear now: "The solar mandala has the following elements: water, fire, air, earth, and ether." We can develop positive mental energy. They're in the music. That's why classical music has always been my precious company. It reduces stress, improves memory, and promotes better sleep. In addition, it lowers blood pressure, as well as enhances emotional intelligence. As it relaxes the body, it helps me meditate. All this. in time, helps me keep an excellent mood.

The project of creating anti-gravity is stalled. We need extra help if we are going to finish this successfully. Bring Tony to help us accomplish this device.

It was Nikola's dream that every human being be born a deity, a divine being that could transcend. Regain consciousness while flying without wings or spacecraft. Awake to the energy contained in the air. Voids in space are simply matter that's not awakened. There's no empty space in this planet or in the universe. Energy was first, followed by matter. Light created everything. Light particles can create the most beautiful symphony. It can take us to the sky.

These sounds are the messages that the universe's harmony is music from stellar heaven. A celestial symphony. I hear it all the time. That's the source of my inspiration. Angels keep observing what is happening on Earth. Aren't those aliens? If you have high awareness, you will see who they are. Guidance from the spiritual energies always helps me. I usually sleep one hour. That's all the rest I need. In my dreams, I find solutions to any problem. I held my inventions in my mind for many years until I realized how to make them come true. Visualization is the most powerful tool I have; an exceptional talent, more than a gift I nurtured.

Diana sends Alina a message. They want to meet you, Tony. Where? It's going to be at the lab. That's where I want to be right now. Mr. Graves himself was waiting for Tony. They dismissed Alina. Even though she had no choice, she didn't want to leave her friend alone. Tony asked, "Who's in charge?" You are from now on. How come? Yes, Tony, you're the lead scientist on this project. Why am I going to work for you? It's your country. I know you're a patriot. What exactly are you doing here? This is the anti-gravity device. Let me see the details. You have full access to all our of resources.

Alina gets a file from Tony. She starts reading. This is a smart file, it changes the language according to my thoughts. It's mind boggling. He's been working on this since he came back home from outer space. He received instructions, not from Nikola. Who could it be? His name is "Barlow." Who's that? I need to read the entire document to get all the information. It mentions "ELO" several times. What does it mean? It doesn't say anywhere. Why did he send this to me? He must be in trouble. Other than Tony, who can help me decipher this? I may ask Nikola about it. He is observing us from afar.

Tony is looking through the eyes of the genius of Nikola. I can see this is wrong. You have the wrong materials. In this non-existent field, we must get rid of all the wiring, you have kilometers of wires in the spacecraft. How do you know it is a spacecraft? You forgot that I have the knowledge of the master of lightning. No, I didn't. However, this is a preliminary version of the device; it doesn't have the shape of the main components yet. It doesn't matter; I know where you're going. You're close to it. Don't branch off. A little detour may make you fail. What other force do we need to combine with gravity? Isn't it obvious, scientists? What is that?

It's electromagnetism. We are going to reverse gravity. How come? Follow my instructions. Aren't we half way? No, not at all. If we removed all the wires, how are we going to get things connected? It's a wireless network, similar to a neural link. Now, it makes sense. What about the cockpit? There's none. How is it going to be piloted? It's simple, by using our minds. You are still missing the most relevant part of this project. What is that if you can tell us? Everything at the right time.

Alina runs to the university. She asks for some professor's name. She found his name on an Internet search. I'm taking my chances by doing this. However, there's not much I can do now. She couldn't find him. He's on vacation, currently abroad. She was disappointed in not reaching this professor. She then called Tony. He answered his cellphone. However, he was under the scrutiny of all eyes in the lab. She said, "I have a couple questions for you." It's not safe for us to talk about it now. Meditate. You will receive the answers through your thoughts. I've never done that. Trust me, you won't need any training, it will come naturally to you. Our friend will guide through.

Alina starts meditating by listening to an audio. I don't think this is going to work. Anyway, I'm going to give it a try. There's nothing else I can do. After a few minutes, she's relaxed, then she hears Nikola's voice. I have some questions for you. I know why you're here. Yes, you've been observing us for a while. That's correct. By the way, who's Barlow? What's ELO? Barlow is one of the old souls, a smart one. Is he alien? That doesn't matter at this level. Regarding entanglement of living organisms,

Tony will know when it is the right time to unveil it. What should I do? Keep the file in a safe place. What about helping? You can contact Tony the same way we're talking right now. That's great.

Anti-gravity is an elusive force. How do you suggest us to manage it? The key particle is graviton, they resonate at a frequency. This is startling. You should wait for more.

Tony is receiving telepathic information from Barlow. Space-time is not as smooth or continuous as you may seem. Hold on a sec! What's it made of? It's made out of pixels. It is pixelated! How can we see that? You have to get to the quantum level, beyond atoms, to get to see the miniscule separation between the subatomic particles. What would we see? Photons or a dark continuous spectrum? This vibration between subatomic particle separations creates gravity! I don't believe it is a result of the separation. You're talking about quantum gravity. It's been drained to other universes. Does it come from another universe or is it produced in ours? Tony was shocked by a wave that knocked him right away. After he fainted, one of the scientists called out his name. He slowly stood up. What happened? I don't know. You must get some rest. You've been under the stress of an unbearably workload. Alright. He walks to his bedroom.

Alina is being chased. She noticed a black SUV tailgating her car. She speeds up to get lost in the traffic. She arrived at her office. She's agitated. What's wrong with you? Somebody is after me. The security guard at the front door walks to the sidewalk to see if there's anybody following her steps. The men came over. Who are you? Get out of our way. Shots were heard. Let's get her. Alina rushed to the elevator. She's going to the eighth floor, which is taking an eternity. However, a few seconds have passed by. She greets the girl at the front desk. The men emerged from a second elevator. They grabbed Alina. One voice said, "Take her away."

Mr. Graves is informed of the latest developments at the base. Do you have a date for the test? Yes, sir. We plan to have the first test of the device tomorrow morning. I'll meet you then. This is going to be a great opportunity to get some leverage with government high ups. They were not expecting these results. I will order more guards to secure the perimeter of the project. I don't want any surprises. Those guys once took advantage of a security breach. It won't happen again. The security chief was instructed to install some laser cannons to prevent any intruders trying to trespass within the base limits.

Tony is conscious now. My head! This is an awful migraine headache. I've never felt anything similar to this. Alina! Where's she? I can reach her. He tries calling her. However, with no results. He tried to contact her telepathically. However, there are no connections. She vanished! She may be in trouble. I've got to get out of here to help her. He tried to get out of the base. Mr. Graves is there. No, Doc. You're not going anywhere. I have to help my friend. We are at the brink of the greatest moment in science. You should be present at the test. Can you locate my friend Alina? Sure, I will make a call to get people working on that issue. Thanks. They are taken to a launching platform. A rocket, a shuttle, and an oval device are in plain sight.

Where's the girl? I don't know. How is that "You don't know"? I asked you to bring her here. We did. Did you kill her? No, not at all. Then where's she? We don't know. A bunch of inept people. You can't do anything without creating some issues. I need people who I can rely on. Mr. Graves contacted Derek at the committee. What can I do for you, Mr. Graves? I think you have in custody someone that is relevant to one of our projects. We don't have anybody. I forgot that you don't do that. Alright, Off the record, where's Alina? I don't know anybody with that name. Listen, Derek. Don't play games with me. Your people have been messy, leaving a track that can be traced to you. Shootings, kidnappings, trespassing a military base, and I could go on for a while. You don't have to. I will get back to you with an answer regarding that person. That's a lot better, thanks. Don't mention it.

Tony is afraid that he may have lost Alina. He sneaks out of the building, then crawls into a hangar. They have a jeep. As he grabbed the key, some steps were heard. On the road, he goes at full speed. He gets to Alina's apartment. Her vehicle is parked there. Then, he decided to go to her office. The receptionist told him what happened. He got the surveillance camera video. Who are these guys? He was disconcerted. He returned to the base. Where have you been? I went to see my friend. Did you get to see her? No, Mr. Graves. He handed the video to him. I will take it from here.

Derek is still questioning his personnel. They are revising videos of Alina's disappearance. This is the video. What's that? It seems to be white noise. Rewind it to see that scene again. Now, pause it right there. Finally, play it back one more time. A few seconds of blurry screen. That's it. She vanished into thin air. What happened there is still a mystery to me.

Tony tries to communicate telepathically with Alina. It seems as if she were dead, in another dimension, or lost in time. Now I can see her through Nikola's eyes. He is taking me to see her. I see Mr. Conti. She's back there at the hotel. Nikola is still there. Oh my!

I desperately looked for Mr. Graves. I shouted at him. He couldn't hear me. I have to figure out how I am going to get her back. I need to get to my lab. Mr. Graves give me my lab back. Why do you want to have those old documents? I don't need to give you reasons. Alright, guys. Give him his trunks. I revised them one by one. It seems I wrote them myself. My eyes moved quickly, scanning the pages for an answer. After hours of searching, I was drained. Moreover, I couldn't believe that they had taken some of his valuable notebooks. I'm going to confront him.

Derek transferred the agents involved in Alina's pathetic kidnapping to another agency. This shameful episode should be erased from our records. Tony calls Derek. I am a scientist working at... Yes, I know who you are. Why are you calling me? Mr. Graves gave me back some of my trunks. However, there are twenty-five crates still missing. I guess you know where they are. I don't share confidential information with civilians. I am the author of such a work. Whoever you are, I don't care. Listen, if I see you face-to-face, you will have to answer my questions. Don't make me laugh. You've been looking for me. Here I am. You're showing you've got guts. Don't flatter me. You made Alina disappear. I have evidence that incriminates your agency. Former agent John had your missing crates in a deposit at an almost abandoned base in Kansas. Send me the location. No, sir. Don't push your luck. That's all you're going to get from me.

The anti-gravity device test was successful. They are all happy, celebrating their accomplishment. It was an excellent addition to the team. That was worth it. Imagine all the things we can do together. The sky is the limit. Tony approaches Mr. Graves. I know where the rest of my chests are located. Where is that? It's in Kansas. Who told you that? I got it straight from the horse's mouth. You mean Derek? Who else? What do you want us to do? Take me to the abandoned military base in Kansas. I need to recover my trunks. They may be vital for future projects. You listened to our lead scientist. Take him right away. Yes, sir. One more thing: you should take your best soldiers with you to guarantee his security. I don't want any unforeseen issues. Rest assured that we'll do as you said.

Derek kept on thinking, "What's so valuable in those old trunks that this scientist wants to recover them?" I doubt they have anything in them. John made sure that they were worthless. I will send some operatives to verify the contents.

It was about time. Tony recovered most of my research. However, he's still tracking the missing ones. My first papers were lost in that unlucky fire.

Although I remembered most of the designs, I didn't have enough time to rewrite my theories or how to accomplish such developments. That's going to be his next task. My soul's with you. Don't be dismayed; hang on tight. We're almost there.

On the way to the base, Tony was thinking of Alina. She's absolutely gorgeous. What I admire the most about her is her convictions. I adore how softly she talks to me, sweet and tender. She has what I didn't have: a family. I'm an orphan who fought for his path in life to get through it. I thrived on conquering what I had. She has faith. I wish I had the same sense of spirituality. Even though I meditate, I'm far from being a devotee of the divine. I'm getting nostalgic. Missing her is bringing me to my knees. I should tell her what I feel for her. My heart is poking out of my chest. This pain is unmeasurable. I must see her again. I know Nikola told me that solitude would be the best partner for an inventor. Science is my passion. However, Alina is my true love. I have to find a way to have both in my life. We arrived at a military airport. There were some people waiting for us. We're going to ride a chopper to the base.

Derek's team was in position on the mountain watching the road. They were warned by the helicopter noise that they were not using ground transportation. They shot a bazooka at the chopper. We hit them. They informed Derek of what they did. Was there a witness? No, there wasn't. Any survivors? No, the helicopter blew up. Proceed with the second stage of the plan. Yes, sir.

Mr. Graves was informed that the helicopter hadn't arrived at its destination. Send some troopers to investigate what happened. I got the news that there was a huge explosion. The helicopter was shot down by some mercenaries. When the rescue team got to the accident area, it was full of debris. No one could have survived this accident. If they had, the fire would have burned them. The search continued and they found the remains of the crew, which had been turned into ashes. Everybody was appalled by the sad news. This is a punch in the gut. We lost the greatest mind of our time.

Derek was fired. Some possible charges are soon to be pressed. He talks to the defense chief. I had no choice. You certainly did. You took your chances, Derek. Now you have to live with the consequences of your actions. Is there any other way I can skip this ordeal? What's coming to you is not well seen by our team. You can vanish in a faraway country under a different identity. You can start over with a clean slate. That sounds great. A reset for me. What about the general attorney? She won't press any charges. I can guarantee you that.

Mr. Graves is trying to locate Derek. He's nowhere. We're tracking him. If we find him, he's going to pay for what he did. His people's reports are disappointing. He received some help. From whom? They must be in the high echelons of government.

Alina is talking to Mr. Conti, trying to find some clues on what Tony was doing in that place. Mr. Conti tells Alina, "They both have brilliant imaginations." Nikola is a master of electricity, while Tony is a young promise, a great scientist in the making. Do you know where they are? Yes, I do.

Nikola is in his basement lab. Tony must be around here. He works part-time at the hotel. In addition, he assists the scientist in his spare time. Let me tell you that they get along well. That's odd. Nikola doesn't enjoy any people around him. He has a few friends. Do you know any of them? Sure, Mark and Guglielmo are frequent visitors. What about Thomas? They used to be close, although now they hardly talk to each other. They've had some issues in the past over some patents. You know, young lady, that money separates. Yes, friendship is similar to money; it's easier to make than to keep. Anything peculiar that you can recall? I usually keep my distance and give him his space to work without any restrictions. I understand. I can show you the way to Nikola's lab. Sure, thanks. If you are lucky, Tony must be with him. His shift has finished. He is either at the lab or running some errands for him. I appreciate your help.

Mr. Graves has been digging around in defense circles since the time device disappeared. John is no longer in this time lapse. Did Derek get access to it? There's no way for me to know that unless I get information from within his organization. I received a message from the search team. Yes, what happened? We have to leave the premises of the accident to the aviation investigation team. They've arrived. This is going to take a few weeks or maybe months. Alright. We're conducting our own investigation.

Alina gets to talk to Nikola. Welcome to my lab. Thank you. I was expecting you. How did you know that I was coming to you? You're a time traveler. You were in my lucid dreams the previous days.

Where's my friend? He's supposed to be there in your time. I'm trying to prevent bad things. I know that. Bear in mind that changing the line of time may cause some disruptions. Thus, unexpected results in the future. Yes, I have to be careful with the changes. What exactly do you have in mind? I want to prevent John from taking your trunks. My belongings? Yes, your papers and inventions are going to be packed into those big containers. How are you going to do that alone? I need to get my hands on his device. How did you get here? I used Tony's backup machine. I see that you are a resourceful young lady. Simply call me Alina. Alright.

Tony is arriving at the hotel. Mr. Conti tells him about a friend who is looking for him. Who's that? It's Alina. Are you kidding me? No, my friend. Where is she? She's at the lab talking to the scientist. Thanks. I'll meet her right away. Wow, he seems pretty excited about her visit. Love is in the air, youth. What a time of life! Tony greets Alina. How is it possible? I had to make a decision. They were going to get rid of me to silence my investigation regarding your work. They wanted to keep things confidential. Listen, I returned after you, Alina. I'm glad to see you. I was involved in a helicopter accident. Well, it was more of an incident created by some dark wings of defense that were trying to get rid of me. I was transported back in time to see you. Wasn't it to escape your death? It was surely a close call. How did you know? I used the time device while I was on the helicopter. I transported myself to the following day. I needed time to prepare my things to come to the beginning of everything. While I was packing my things, I was on the news. They think that I died. It was a deliberate attack. They both hugged. Tony told her, "I love you, Alina." That's why I am here. I love you too. Nikola interrupted them. There's no time for love now. We have more urgent matters to solve at this moment.

I knew it. Derek was abroad with a different identity. He was a spy. I guess you are for life. His whereabouts are soon to be revealed to us.

We have to get to your effects before anybody else's. You have to go on your own. Why? I cannot leave this place, even though my time here is almost over. Alright, we understand. Alina Tony rushed to the old terminal to get to Nikola's belongings. How much time do we have? Not much. John is going to be here in less than an hour. Tony started uncovering some devices, including a small tower. What are you doing? I'm getting ready to welcome the thieves. They will have the time of their lives. What are we going to do? We are going to give them a taste of the master's work. Last time, when I got here, somebody had been through all the documents. Yes, I can see that most of the trunks had already been sealed. Some of them were still here. Now it is a completely different story. Everything is here. These are one of the most controversial documents in history. The perfected beam of death is among the designs. There are technical papers that will make a difference for humankind. Here's the precious manuscript. A manuscript? Yes, it is Nikola's notebook, with several hundred pages of scribbles, designs, notes, and comments handwritten by the master of light.

Government authorities marked some of those pages as strictly confidential. They are not to be shared under any circumstances due to the nature of their contents. What's in those pages? Weaponry out of this world, anti-gravity devices, wireless technology, among other far-fetched technologies.

Listen, some steps are approaching us. Let's be quiet. They are not going to seize this place the way they did before. They have no interest in preserving these documents for future generations. All they want to do is hide them or use them selectively. Did they analyze the paper? No, they didn't. The personnel they used were not capable of such a feat.

A small army swarmed the narrow tunnels of the old metro station. Are we going to talk to them? No, there's no reason for such a dumb movement. They listen to the guards getting closer. His leader signaled to a machine room. He knows where the documents are. Tony moves a handle that triggers the mechanism of the tower. Millions of volts were all over the place. The guards were perplexed. The lead agent told them to continue. Tony opened the sewage that brought a small river, which was running free in the tunnel. The enormous voltage catapulted the electrification of those intruders.

Derek is skiing in the mountains. A girl calls him "Jean." Come over here. They both laugh while walking to the restaurant at the top of the mountain. A couple is on their honeymoon in a snow resort. Mr. Graves is following his most recent clue. They told me he was in a small town on Mount Blanc. It's a matter of time. I'll find him.

Chief, some news regarding Jean. What's that? A friend of yours is chasing him. Mr. Graves? Yes, sir. Has he been successful? No, not yet. However, he's getting dangerously close. Don't let him. I know he's on a mission with a vengeance.

Are we going to pack all the documents? No, not all of them. Let's take those files that were censored by the government. We have to leave most of the trunks. Thus, they will have something to confiscate. Hurry up Alina, I'm sure that more agents will show up to see what happened to their friends. Do we have to take the safe box with us? If we could open it, then it wouldn't be necessary. I know what he knew. Yes, I completely forgot that odd connection. That's kind of complicated. These safe boxes were used as a receptacle for storing valuables or documents. The papers are well-preserved. Do you have the combination to open it? I can infer it; knowing Nikola's obsession with number 3, I can follow my gut. Tony starts with the combination of 3 left, 6 left, 9 right, 18 left, 36 right, got it! Let's see what's inside.

Mr. Graves notices a man is looking at him. I've seen him before. He may have been chasing me. I pretend I'm going to the restroom. I will open the window. He put on a cap. Then he reversed his coat. This is a two-color version, handy for any special occasion.. He merged into the crowd at the resort. I think I confused him. While the man was entering the restroom, he noticed one window was open. He called somebody to let him know. They are breathing on my neck. I must be careful. Mr. Graves gets some backups to protect him while searching for Derek.

Nikola guided me to take these documents, including his beloved notebooks, to a safe location.

I thought there was one. That's what most people think, anyway. The authorities did an excellent job. These files contain valuable information, leading to breakthroughs in science. How much time have we been here? The time elapsed is not relevant; we can return to our current timeline. I am keen on studying the research he was engaged in in his last years. We have lots of unpublished work in these containers. I have to determine whether these manuscripts contain any incendiary material or they were taken into custody for political reasons. What was behind those decisions may be a mystery we won't be able to unravel unless we enquire the right people. We are not going back to any of these guys. They won't tell us the truth. They have no reason for doing that. Do you think that by taking these containers, history is going to be changed? Yes, it will be changed. However, it will be a subtle change. We took what was banned. They didn't use it after all.

Mr. Graves spotted Derek around the resort. He sent some of his agents to him. He was not surprised. You are mistaken, gentlemen. I'm Jean. They didn't talk to him, they went directly to grab him. Later, they took him to a cabin away from the resort. Welcome to our humble home. Why did you bring me here? You are aware of what you did. You destroyed our property, killed our scientist and the rest of the crew. All the damage you inflicted on me, our project, and our country is not going to be forgiven. Hey, Mr. Graves, listen up. There's something much bigger than this going on. What's that? I cannot tell you. Then shut up. Our government is out of control. Why do you say that?

They disregard all the rules I've been trained on. They're explicitly inconsistent with regard to acknowledging aliens or their technology, even though they use reverse engineering to replicate their devices and spacecraft. Where are you going with this? The chief is flat out illegal. What is worse, he doesn't even care about it. That's why you are here. You see, the kind of decoupling that exists between Ma'am President and her staff is really concerning. Her policies should be connected to her actions. There's no logic; we're going down the rabbit hole. Protecting you, Derek, is a perverse incentive to enhance bad practices. You are responsible for amplifying torture, kidnappings, and killings. You see, nobody cares right now. The search for Tony tarnishes Nikola's legacy in a way that controls superior technology. The scientist and his team can vanish at any time. It is hard for me to reconcile such policies. I do care for my people. You've shown incompetence, Mr. Graves. How dare you say that? You are too blind to see the truth. What is that? There's an ulterior political motive. Truth is fungible and disposable to some corrupt politicians. Power needs alien technology to dominate other nations. This is not a race between espionage and science. Tony is not dead! Are you kidding me? No, I am not. He was not in the helicopter. I saw him when he got on. He got off at some point. The analysis of the remains, including DNA, didn't find any samples containing his. This is overwhelming. What are you doing here? I have a house, horses, a farm, and another life. This is my retirement. I have done too much for my country. Therefore, I now deserve something back. No, you don't. You have to pay for those killings. My people didn't have to die because of your deadly practices. I'm here because they don't want to seek attention. This recent accident has been an issue for them.

Tony and Alina arrived safely at Tony's apartment. We brought back the three time devices. John won't be able to come back to the future. He's going to stay in his timeline, where he belongs. By the way, where are we going to keep all these documents? Let's rent a truck. Are we going to take them away? Yes, we have to keep them away from those that may want to get their hands on them. Any suggestions? Yes, I have an aunt who has a house by the lake. Let's do it. They brought the truck. It took a lot of effort to load six heavy trunks. Alina calls her aunt to let her know that she's going to pass by. She was glad to hear from her.

Alina is an investigative reporter. She has a science blog in which she keeps her readers informed on the latest developments. What's her involvement with the scientist? Sir, I think they are a couple. Where is she? She fled from one of our detention locations. When was that? That was yesterday. Why haven't you recaptured her? She vanished in front of our eyes. Are you still mesmerized by some magic trick? You can search anywhere; don't return without her. Yes, chief. The least we want is some loose ends out there. We are meticulous with our work; this is not a moment to show any weaknesses or start being messy. I must get things straightened out at once.

Oil companies, electricity distributors, and the energy industry in general are pulling the strings.

They don't want, under any circumstance, this device that would make wireless electricity affordable, to take over and ultimately ruin their businesses. The pressure is huge. Government authorities don't want that either. Millions of dollars in taxes will be lost, along with jobs as well. This is not a political move. It may be eco-friendly, meaning progress, sustainability, and zero emissions of carbon dioxide. However, it is more than a headache for us. Making electricity universally available is disturbing.

Tony has called Mr. Graves. However, he couldn't reach him. He decided to go to the base to continue with his work. Alina will stay behind for a while, or at least until things settle down. When Tony gets to the base entrance, the soldiers are stunned by his presence. He greeted them, then continued to his lab. The rest of the scientific team came to see him as soon as they got the news. What happened to you? That's a long story. Please tell us. I didn't get on the helicopter because I had forgotten part of my gear. I told the pilot to take the rest of my things with him. I was going to get there by plane. Why didn't you show up before? I had an accident, which is why I couldn't make it either. I was at the hospital four hundred miles from here. How did you get there? I don't recall that part. I'm glad to see you're alive. Thanks, I'm back to work. Where's Mr. Graves? He's on a trip. When is he coming back? We don't know. You can call him. I've already done it. Don't worry, he will soon call you back.

Meanwhile, Alina is in the basement organizing the documents in the different trunks. He wants me to sort these files by year and then by topic. It's going to take me a long time to do that. Anyway, I don't have anything else to do right now. Shall I call the newspaper? I'd better wait a couple of days. What's this, Auntie? That's an old cistern. It's been a while since we last used it. Do you have anything in mind? Yes, I was thinking about using it to store these trunks. It is a dry and secure location for storing and preserving documents and electronic devices. Sure, that's a great idea. You need to clean it. After that it will be a perfect fit. Alina continues organizing the pile of documents. These papers are from the safe. She comes across some papers with the design of a weapon. Nikola has conceived a torpedo with anti-gravity propulsion. This is more of a rocket or a spacecraft than a missile. It has the design, some mathematical formulas, the specifications, and the details of how to construct such a spaceship. It has a note: "Do whatever it takes to preserve this breakthrough. Humankind may depend on it in the near future." What does it mean? I don't have the faintest idea. I'm going to record everything on video. I'll make it public when the time is right.

The government was vitally interested in anti-gravity. Mr. Graves, Derek, John, and the defense chief, among others, have been actively involved in the pursuit of this technology. Tony started the construction of the device without any prior knowledge. He's been guided by the master of light. I will place these blue prints against the wall. Every precaution is well-justified. We must protect them from any robbers, including foreign governments.

Derek and Mr. Graves returned to their country. A meeting with the defense chief is out of the question. I don't want to see his face. What is going to happen to me? You are going to be judged according to what you've done. You cannot do that to me. Why not? I mean, you know that everything I did was for our nation. Put an end to that story. Your rhetoric is not going to work with me.

Operatives are frantically looking for Nikola's late work. The defense chief raised the question that after the safe was opened right after his death, some of its supposed contents were not found. Now, it is the right time to search for it. The scientist must know where it is. He claims he knows everything that Nikola knew. Where's he? He's working on a special project with Mr. Graves. Bring him to me. What about the project? You have to do whatever it takes to do it. I couldn't care less about Mr. Graves' experiments.

Tony is in awe. No further action has been taken since we returned. Alina is back at her office. She received an assignment. Pro Science is protesting in front of Congress, asking congressmen to declassify all of Nikola's documents. She tells her team to merge among the protesters. Later, she runs into Leon. He is there as part of the group. She asked him, "What's going on here?" This is huge, my friend. What does Pro Science do? It is an organization in the namer of Nikola. Who are your members? Our members are people who are closely associated with studying Nikola's achievements and honor his contributions to humankind. What about you? I have personally studied his documents regarding electromagnetism. I feel it is fair to perpetuate Nikola's work. We must do something to recognize what he did for the world. Why are you here today? We are pushing for a total declassification of the master's documents. Do you think they are going to pay attention to your group? Yes, this is the right time to pressure them. Why do you think this time they will pay attention to you? It's simple. Elections are in a couple of weeks. That's why they want to please people to get their votes. I hope you have an interest in the organization. What about your friend, Alina? Who? The scientist. Ah, Tony. Yes, what is he doing? He intends to undertake some of Nikola's unfinished work in the near future. He's currently working on an anti-gravity project. He initiated that project on behalf of the master. If you don't mind my asking, Is he still in contact with Nikola's consciousness? He has a great understanding of his mind. I could say that he sees through Nikola's eyes.

Operatives spotted Alina at the protest. They approached her. She moved quickly as soon as she noticed them. They tried to take her away. However, Leon and his peers noticed the men. This created a riot. Shots were fired. Then a stampede came over the agents. Alina barely escaped, thanks to her friends. The news reported a violent protest. Organizers blamed the infiltration of agents that disrupted the peaceful demonstration.

Tony was aware of what was going on. They are coming after us. Nikola, what should I do? Don't run away, use my devices to get their attention, don't negotiate with any intermediary. You should get to the president.

Alina is scared. The organization saved her this time. She keeps in touch with them. The members set up a system of sharing information among them. She got the news that the defense chief was after them. Furthermore, there are some members of Pro Science that are of interest to them too. Herewith, one set of the documents was hidden beneath the floor. Part of our heritage was rescued.

A comprehensible account was attached to the message we sent you earlier today. What's all that about? We are going to transfer one of your scientists. Who? Doctor Tony. Why? It is in the best interests of our nation. No way. I won't accept that. You can escalate it to whomever you want. However, that won't work this time. I know of all your schemes. They have harmed science. That's nonsense. You know better than that. This is war, chief! The tension among these top officials is reaching a boiling point. The mediator is Ma'am President. However, she doesn't think that she needs to get involved in such matters. She believes in the independence of power. Her staff should be capable of making decisions without consulting with her, unless it is a case of national security, in which her involvement is a must.

Alina and Tony decided to make a genuinely unexpected move. Let's meet the defense chief. Mr. Graves was invited to go with them. He agreed to accompany them. He suggested meeting that powerful man in neutral territory. Where is that? Don't worry, I know how to handle this situation. The wheels of counter-espionage are turning. What does that mean, Mr. Graves? It means that unsolicited help is coming to you. They moved to a hotel close to the border. Agents are sneaking into the nearby rooms.

Nikola used to walk alone. There's one Nikola. The unique master of lightning. Now we're together. This conversation among Pro Science members takes place before a meeting to decide the course of action for the organization. It is imperative to advertise its agenda on social media. It is going to request public aid to fund its activities. Who's going to fund these punks? Sir, most of them are brilliant scientists. They are gaining traction among young activists. Authorities are observing their moves closely. They may raid their offices at any time.

A large sum is now being sought through people's goodwill. This campaign is conducted to help defray the mortgage on the property on which Pro Science has its facilities. The members hope to raise the necessary money to pay off the debt. Alina made a modest transfer to their account. It's the least I can do for them after their rescue.

The defense chief, escorted by his entourage, is entering the hotel. They took control of the entrance. elevators, service areas, and emergency exits. Tony asked if this was an ambush. It's not time for fear, my friend. We are in this situation now. My people are holding their positions. There's nothing left to chance. I'm glad to hear that.

The fund for Pro Science is an outgrowth of a plea that resulted in the wake of the last meeting of the organization. Any pledge made by a corporation is not enough to cover our expenses, which are growing by the minute. To avoid paying taxes, these companies merely offer their crumbs. That's why we are going overseas to look for better results. Our organization is as poor as a church mouse.

The defense chief, Casper, enters the meeting room, followed by his assistant. While Alina, Tony, and Mr. Graves were waiting for them. Some agents stayed outside the door. Save all the formalities, let's go straight to the point. Hand in the files, as well as any inventions you possess, Tony. I am willing to do it with one stipulation before I divulge it to you. What's that? I would continue working on the project at the base. I can decide to take up your offer right away. However, I don't trust you since you've been at large. I came to you voluntarily. Isn't it a gesture of good-will? You're smart, my friend. If I take your word, it may harm my career. Mr. Graves added, "I see you didn't come here to negotiate." For your information, Casper, my people have taken over as your agents. You no longer hold any advantage over us. I should have expected that from you. To the best of my knowledge, you have some devices that are literally out of this world. Tell me about them. You know what I am talking about. The existence or non-existence of such devices is merely speculative. You're the one that can confirm or deny that. Some helicopters are flying over the hotel. Are you going to start a war in downtown to get what you want. Tony threw a key to Casper. Go to this address. There you will find the safe box with the missing documents. In addition, you may find some machines that do exist. One more thing: don't come after us. Is that a threat? How are we going to do that to the defense chief? Mr. Graves said, "Let's go to the roof using the elevator." A helicopter is waiting for us.

The construction of a death beam plant is a recent project that the military is about to embark on. They are going to use the documents facilitated by Tony. He furnished us with the information we wanted to receive. Our adversaries won't get hold of any of Nikola's ideas. Some machines that were confiscated are unknown to our scientists. It's going to take them some time to figure out how they function. Let's reclassify them as top secret until further notice. That seems to be the right thing to do, since this man was at least one or two centuries ahead of his time. Yes, the prodigal genius of Nikola left us a heritage. The world-famous inventor's documents, as well as his machines, will be safe in our vault.

It is disheartening to see how someone who's supposed to protect us and is entrusted to uphold scientific breakthroughs just mocks scientists along with the system. He's going to seal those documents unless some young politicians stop him. If they decide to use the manuscript, they will encounter a challenge in deciphering Nikola's torturous handwriting. Although he wrote in English, his penmanship was small, blurry, or perhaps difficult to understand.

Tony tells his friends, "We have great designs to be developed." Which ones? Ball lightning propulsion, which involves electro-gravity, is a revolutionary design for a spaceship. A plasma confinement technique for fusion reactors, which sets up waves on Earth's surface. What are you going to get your hands on first? It will definitely be a fusion energy design in which ball lightning is the key element. We're going to attempt to artificially replicate a 20 million volt storm. This is similar to the fusion power used by stars. Magnetic confinement along with laser implosions may be painstakingly achieved. I will use a glowing sphere of plasma against a strong wind. This will show a recently discovered state of matter: plasma. This hitherto unknown concept of matter is something recent.

Many of the ablest minds of this era are trying to devise ways in which we can get use of Nikola's inventions. They are competent to some extent. Although they prefer to be punitive, they censor or hide these creations. Why is that? It is intended not to shadow their prestige with a lack of expertise in what was once the knowledge of the master of light on a daily basis.

Alina asked Tony, Did Nikola have love in his life? Besides his love for science, pigeons have their share. I guess there was no woman who could compete with them. I remember the story of a girl who had a crush on Nikola. Who was that? It was Anne. I haven't heard of her. She was J.P.'s daughter, a friend of his. Did he love her? He was fond of her in a platonic way. Did they have any dates? The closest thing must have been a dinner at her parents' house. Nikola paid more attention to the cubic shape of a dessert than to that young lady. That was rude! That was basically him. Although he was married to science, he was a romantic who even wrote some poetry when he was young. Did he publish any poetry books? Unfortunately, he didn't. He kept that side of his personality to himself. Some of his poems are seen in some of his letters, though. There was another woman, Katherine. A celebrity that was close to the master. A man of many close calls, catastrophic events, misfortune, and even lucky encounters. What do you mean by "lucky encounters"? He met Mark, J.P., Thomas, George, Charles, and Guglielmo, among other authorities and celebrities.

Mr. Graves, Alina, and Tony were taken hostage by Casper. Send them to the dungeons. This is illegal. It is a matter of national security. If you are going to disguise your actions under that umbrella, that's not going to work. The whole project was dismantled. The anti-gravity devices, including the prototype, were taken to an undisclosed location. The employees were reassigned to other roles. No questions were answered. They had no choice other than to obey his orders. The documents were again buried among the bulk of materials gathered throughout decades of censorship that covered-up alien reverse engineering.

Tony contacted Leon to let him know what had happened to them. The organization is ready to protest to request a disclosure of the hideous operations performed by the defense chief. Furthermore, they will request the freedom of their friends. The headquarters of Pro Science were raided by police officers. The building was evacuated and sealed as a crime scene for investigation, even though nothing happened there. The members of the organization were arrested. They have been questioned regarding Nikola's documents. Moreover, they want to establish their link with Tony's project. It was revealed that their contact was mostly with Alina, who had little to do with the late genius of Nikola. They are defending science not politics. They will not press charges after all.

Alina was set free after she revealed the location of the missing documents, which were hidden under a barn. The agents destroyed her aunt's barn and house in search of any device. Alina is reunited with her aunt; they are both at her apartment. This is over for us. What about Tony? I don't know what they are going to do with him.

The defense chief has to report to the president what has been going on. Ma'am President. Casper. Everything has been done as you instructed us. The scientist is a liability. Why? He's suffering from amnesia. Experts say it is the result of mental exertion. He began to become forgetful. Now it is more than an irregular pattern. Send him to a mental institution under our care.

Tony arrived at the asylum. I am out of prison. However, I am in this mad house. Alina is talking to the doctor. What's wrong with Tony? He's having language, problem-solving, keeping track of things, and other thinking issues. Is this serious? It is severe enough to interfere with his daily life. Is he going to get better? We still need to run a round of tests to see what exactly is affecting him. There are some abnormal brain changes. He's not the same, Doc. What do you mean? He shows odd behavior. In addition, he doesn't express any feelings when he sees me, That's affecting our relationship. You have to be patient.

This is the best place for me right now. The automatism of life, monotony, and boredom are my best friends these days. I need to get relief from this cosmic pain. I will rise from my ashes. They will see what they have done. The world won't be the same again.

After the revision, Alina comes to talk to the doctor, who is concerned that Tony may have a personality disorder. What are his symptoms? He thinks he's another person. He shows pervasive distrust as well as suspicion of other people, an unjustified belief that others want to harm him. Besides his lack of interest in social interaction or relationships, his eccentric behavior displays an inability to feel pleasure from the simple things in life. That's true, doctor. He doesn't enjoy humor because he doesn't understand jokes. Additionally, he has an odd perception. He tells us that he hears voices or talks to aliens. He's close to delirium, attributing to himself magic powers of materializing his thoughts, which affect reality. Furthermore, he's a perfectionist who neglects his family or friends to get his work perfectly done. Some of the symptoms indicate a paranoid personality disorder. Besides his mental condition, we have to treat some damage due to diathermy. What's that? Those burns on his skin were produced by deep heat under his skin. Any idea what may have caused that? He had been at his lab carrying out some experiments with electricity in which he exposed himself to high voltages. I almost forgot to tell you, Alina, that he occasionally shows some cruelty trend, some sort of compulsive drive.

I'm bitterly complaining about people ingratitude and unfairness. I am weary of bickering and backbiting. I'm aching due to all the projects I am running simultaneously. I have to clear my mind. They say I am crazy. Who isn't? I am little

74

confused because I am not seeing through Nikola's eyes. It is more assuming his personality than anything else. That's troublesome.

Is the scientist feeling better? No, sir. He's getting worse. He's somehow possessed. He claims that he was visited by an alien entity. That could be possible since he was previously abducted. He said that he had been communicating with an entity from Mars. That's the reason he was going to travel to Mars. I wouldn't doubt it either. What about acting or talking as if he were Nikola? That's something pretty different, my friend. He needs to rest following his treatment.

Alina is in the courtyard talking to Tony. Are you feeling better? Yes, I am. However, it's better if they think that I am still having mental issues. Why is that? I cannot tell you now. Here, the walls have ears. There are many cameras around us. What are we going to do? I will see what happens tonight. That's fantastic. Keep it quiet. Alright. Alina heads home. Who's going to help him? Whoever it is, I will know soon. Mr. Graves came to see Tony. I know you are fine. You don't have to fake it with me. Anyway, I am your friend. Yes, you are. I got the project, all the equipment, and the personnel. The matchless missing piece is you. That's fascinating. How did you do that? I have some connections in my friend's network. I see you are determined to continue with this research. Have you seen this? No, I haven't. What's that? See if for yourself. It's a manuscript. No, Tony. Look at it again. It's Nikola's diary. Yes, it is. Even though it is challenging to understand his penmanship. We identified some relevant devices. Which ones?

Some high-tech prototypes. Is this the original document? No, it isn't. It is just a copy. You can keep it. Sure.

Casper gets a notification. What's this? A red flag from the asylum. What's the matter? Graves. I'm on my way. When Casper gets there, the visitation hours were over. He demanded to see the director. The nurse told him that he was not in the facilities. He ignored her and entered the director's office. How dare you to enter my office? Who are you? He managed to convince the director, who reluctantly allow him to see the patient for five minutes. Trust me, it won't take more than that. Hey, Tony. Do you remember me? Yes, doctor. I am not your doctor. What did Graves give you? That's an ugly suit! If you are playing games with me, that won't work out. Casper called the nurse. Take him back to his room. He goes after them. As soon as the nurse leaves, Casper enters the room 72. He is looking for the notebook. Where is it? Tony didn't reply and hit the alarm. All the nurses and personnel came to see what was going on. He turns violently throwing objects. They asked Casper to leave right away. Peace returned to the area as soon as the man in black turned his back. His presence alters the patient. He shouldn't be allowed to see him again.

The doctor in service came to check on the patient. Tony was subdued and snoozed. Too many ideas go through his head. That man should have told him something that ignited that anger burst. This is going to delay his recovery. They left him sleeping on his bed. He opened his eyes and got dressed. He had placed the notebook at the front desk among other medical books before the undesired visitor. He walks quickly and takes it back. Now it is time to hit the road.

Tony knocks at Alina's door. How did you get here. I walked from the hospital, my darling. I'm happy to see you. I need my communication equipment. It's in the basement. What do you need it for? I am receiving messages from Mars. Who's contacting you? Barlow. Who's that? It's a superior being. He's helping me transcend. Although telepathy is weak, I was able to successfully retrieve part of the message. It may be perceived as nonsense since we are missing portions of it.

This equipment exceeds the requirements for communication with Mars. There's no other place in this galaxy that's better than Earth. My beautiful sweetheart, this is a once in a lifetime opportunity. There are no limits. Those men are still hunting you. They will come after you. It doesn't matter anymore. It's been a while since I haven't seen you happy, Tony. Listen, my love. Barlow will provide us with the knowledge to eliminate hunger on Earth, control weather and seismic tectonic plates, limitless energy, and a direct communication with his race. Martians? They are our ancestors. Wow! I foresee a better future.

The director of the asylum was informed that a patient escaped during the night. Who was that? It was Tony. Let's inform the authorities about it. When Casper got the news he was stunned. This man is unpredictable. A manhunt was ordered. They surrounded Alina's apartment. Tony used an oscillator, which triggered a local earthquake. Police officers were astonished by the impact. As it intensifies, buildings start to shake. A nearby bridge collapsed. While on the other side, it was not trembling. How is it possible that a few meters away, all this destruction is happening such a disaster? I don't know why it is not perceived on this side. This must an artificial tremor. He must have some device that is producing this. The wreckage left debris on the road, which provided the distraction for them to escape. Where are we going, Tony? Don't worry. We're moving to safe ground away from these men.

Casper was aware of the powerful device that was activated. It is incredibly destructive. His whereabouts are unknown. A desperate operation was in progress to capture them. Alina tells, "How are we going to get out of this." It may sound suicidal. However, I have a plan to get to Mars. You will stay behind with your aunt. They won't do anything to you. The launch is early in morning. I have the spacecraft ready. I even have a robot vehicle to explore the martian terrain. There's one more thing I need to complete the plan. What's that? Mr. Graves has to help me get to the base. Once there, I'll get on the spacecraft. Do you think that he is going to help you? Yes, of course. He came to me at the hospital to offer some help, as much as he could. This is quite different. He's going to be in hot water if he helps you. I will give him the automatic mechanisms that will cement the basis for future robotics. Automatic beings? Yes, a revolution of science. I called him and we're going to meet at the base. Alina kissed him goodbye.

He made the first mistake. What was that? He called Graves. Perfect. Where's he? He's on the way to the base. Send all the troops to that location. I will see there.

Mr. Graves is anxiously awaiting Tony. Headlights in the distance are approaching the base. In addition, helicopters and patrols are all over the place. Hurry, let's get inside. Take me to the spacecraft. This is a reckless act; we won't survive. That's not going to happen, trust me. Take the oscillator to give them a warm welcome. Mr. Graves pushed the button. Then the vibration created a seismic cataclysm. This way, beyond this door there it is. I almost forgot, here is the file with the robotics designs. I wish you luck. Same to you, buddy. Casper was shaken. However, he and his soldiers entered the military base. Where's he? He's at the backyard. Tony! Surrender! There's nothing you can do! He didn't reply. He took off. In a few seconds, his spacecraft disappeared. Mr. Graves told Casper what he had confiscated. The files contain the robotics designs, weather and seismic controls, as well as a prototype of the martian vehicle. They were left behind by Tony. At least we're not empty handed.

Mr. Graves was taken to be questioned regarding the incident at the base. There was nothing we could do. Not even you, Casper. What do you mean? Not even the powerful defense chief could stop this man. That's not a man. That's an alien entity disguised as a human. He possesses superpowers we don't even imagine. Where did he go? I guess he went to Mars.

Alina was reading the notebook that she'd kept. It is based on the principles of studying a microscopic world. I know he's going to meet

Nikola, the hurler of lightning. It is possible the presence of an entity in an encounter in outer space, and here I am, small and lonely.

A paramount component in the communication with Tony is going to be this crystal, to magnify the signal. As I held it in my hands, it lit up. The light was bright enough that it covered the entire area of the farm and further. A few minutes later, I got the news that there was a global blackout. The whole planet? Yes, the entire globe. Leon came to tell Alina about the organization. We are all proud that you both are part of us. Do you have any idea of what may have triggered the global blackout? It may be some experimental weapon the government is testing.

Scientists at the lab were trying to figure out some of the designs when the blackout took place. What happened? We don't know. What about the emergency generators? Nothing's working. All the machines are dead. It is the same all over the world. Mass hysteria took over. It was madness. Some lightning struck several buildings. After that, everything was quiet. This is odd. I was admiring the calm after the storm. Nikola's face was on a cloud. Next to it, there was Tony's. The same scene repeated around the world. Was electricity restored? No, not at all. Where is that light coming from? Some countries are reporting sun light at night. People are thrilled by this sunlight. That's not sunlight, it is electricity. Wireless electricity. Free electricity for all. The message is clear: A glow around the planet is visible. Where does it come from? We are still searching any possible source.

Ma'am President. I am awestruck. This man is genuinely a mastermind out of his time. Who? Nikola. What about Tony? Now I don't know who's who.

Pro Science is having a celebration that has received the support of many other organizations around the world. This is the beginning of our freedom. Technology for all and for everything. They had banners requesting the use of the oscillator for controlling earthquakes. Some other people were singing and dancing.

Little did they know. Nikola invented a time machine. Alina. Our government had tried to recreate his time machine for over decades. Did you succeed? Yes, we did. However, the results were disastrous. Did Tony talk to you about time traveling? Yes, of course, Mr. Graves. He did travel to the past to fix some mistakes. That's staggering. Yes. That's fantastic. Many people perished in our attempts of achieving time travel. We had to cancel the project until further research came available. Where did Tony travel? He traveled to Nikola's time to learn from the genius. The mad scientist as he was called, was right. We were wrong. We know that he traveled to the future to acquire endless knowledge. We inferred that he could travel to other planets to be exposed to other civilizations. I agree with you. Nikola found a window in time therefore he was able to travel to the past and into the future. Space-time was not a limit to him. Do you think that Tony is coming back? I know that he will be back soon. Who has the documents regarding time travel? Those are still classified materials. As well as the invisibility shield. That's the electromagnetic ring that makes objects undetectable to radars. It creates the green mist, an illusion of invisibility. You know about them. Those documents were retrieved by Tony. It had terrible effects on the crew aboard the ship. What happened to them? Many of them fainted, others suffered mental health issues afterwards. Additionally, some even died instantaneously. There are rumors of odd disappearances. Those are not rumors. Some soldiers were lost in time or another dimension. We never knew what happened to them. It was the consequence of dealing with a technology unknown to them. Most of the soldiers didn't know what they were doing. They connected the wires all over the ship.

There's a recent project, Mr. Graves. It is top secret. We have to stop the tests to avoid unwanted results. They won't listen to you, Alina. At least I need to try. They will imprison you. Alina was disappointed with Mr. Graves. Then she goes to Leon to get help from his friends at Pro Science. She tells them all the details. Let's organize a protest in front of Congress to let them know what is going on.

Casper and Mr. Graves are weighing the pros and cons of the time machine. It doesn't matter what happens. We have to sacrifice ourselves for our nation. Progress demands such patriotic deeds. It is going to get creepier than anything we've seen before. They are making all the arrangements for the test tomorrow. Ignore the protests. Those are terrorist groups; they complain about everything. We have to develop this machine, otherwise a foreign government may take advantage of us. If they are the first to have access to this technology, it could have harmful consequences for all of us.

The test is ready to start. Scientists were instructed to complete their tasks without disclosing the nature of the experiment. The crew is connecting wires all over the ship. They are unaware of what is about to happen. As they push the button to ignite the machine, a green mist covers the sea around the ship. Even though it is fading away, you can still see the water moving, creating waves, that are the result of a ship moving at high speed on the sea. The entire ship vanished in front of our eyes. They received a call. It has rematerialized six hundred kilometers ahead. However, fifteen minutes into the past. How's the group? We're going to have a report in a few minutes. Some were wrecked by microwaves. Many are suffering from schizophrenia due to the trauma caused by this experiment. Some soldiers had terrible injuries. In what was a horrifying scene, some soldiers materialized embedded in the ship's walls, partially into the walls. That's something to be forgotten.

Leon asked Alina if she thought that the project Philadelphia would continue. Not with that name. Intelligent beings from a neighboring planet are sending messages. Can you translate them? I have some gadget that can help us understand what they are sending. Alina says, "Warning, you are going beyond your understanding. You're doomed." Anything else? No. What did they refer to? I have a hint. Who? I supposed they refer to the time machine project results. I will send the message to the government and to the media. Great idea, that way they won't be able to deny it.

Tony descended upon his lab. It feels fine to be back. He calls Alina. She's elated to see him again. We're going to expose the time machine project. I have videos of the experiment. That's impressive. We'll do it together. Leon, using his leverage at Pro Science, is helping me. I know, they are welcome come along. Do you know where the message came from? Yes, I do. Venus? No. Mars? Yes. Why are you monosyllabic? I am thinking on the things we are going to do tomorrow. Nicola confided that to me. Are you going to tell me what you did all this time in outer space? Yes, of course. The boldness of their vision got me flabbergasted. It is magnificent. What did you answer? I told them, "Rest undoubtedly that I would find a way to get to government authorities."

The encounter at the government house is in a few minutes. Tony, Alina, Leon, and a special guest are led to the meeting room. Ma'am President. Finally, I met you, doctor. Who is in your entourage? My fiancée, Alina, our friend Leon, from Pro Science. Oh, they are such a headache for my government. And he's Barlow!

Casper, Derek, and Mr. Graves were done cleaning up the mess of the failure. The time machine works. However, we need to find ways to protect people to avoid such losses. Casper and Mr. Graves are in a hurry. A helicopter is taking them to the reception. What are they celebrating? They are not celebrating anything at all. The president invited Tony to add him to our team. As they climbed up the flight of stairs, they noticed that people were agitated. Most of them were rushing to the main room. What's going on? Something happened inside. What? I don't know. They all ran to the door. As they passed the door, they noticed that giant figure in the middle of the room had green skin, an elongated head, and big eyes. He says, "I'm a peace ambassador." The president made a gesture to her security to remain posted.

Breaking news: "An alien meets the president." Tony brought a surprise to the meeting. A special guest that has the world heads over heel. Are you fine, Ma'am President? Yes, of course. We have to take it with a grain of salt. All the visitors were dismissed. Tony and Barlow were conducted to another room. Alina demanded to stay, and so did Leon. However, they were both sent out of the government house. Tony told her, "Ma'am, you'd better bring Alina and Leon back." Is this a threat? It's a request. She nods her head, and they were brought back. Are you satisfied now? Yes, Ma'am. Thanks for the courtesy. What is all this about? We have a message? From whom? His civilization. Would you mind introducing yourself? In a hoarse voice, Barlow says, "I'm the fifth generation of observers. I am the regent of the Martian underground base. Don't you have people on the surface? No, the radiation doesn't allow us to live on the surface. Why haven't you contacted us before? We have done it. However, you didn't understand our messages. You confused them with black hole waves, solar wind, background white noise, and many other known phenomena to you. Are you originally from Mars? No, I am not. Our civilization resides in a distant galaxy. We are the outpost for helping planetary civilizations thrive in this vast cosmos. Even though the president was nervous, she managed to maintain an undisturbed posture.

Casper joined the meeting. Sorry, I arrived a little late. I was solving some issues of national security. We know the mess you were in. How dare you use such alien technology? I was doing this on behalf of our country. Keep it quiet, Casper. Barlow looks at him. You are the reason why I am here. You selfish, irresponsible beings have disrupted space-time. It created such an unbalance that our world is in peril. I don't know what you are talking about. Do you know where your people are? Some of them are lost. No, they aren't. They are in between dimensions. Casper ordered, "Arrest them." Barlow used antigravity; thus, all the people in the room were pressed against the ceiling. Don't be a fool. You can't hurt me. Do you think that I'm coming this far to be easily stopped by your soldiers? Casper couldn't answer since his mouth was against one of the big lamps.

Barlow paralyzed the president. Then, he asked her to sign some executive orders regarding space diplomacy as a leverage tool throughout conflict. Laws regarding restrictions on the use of nuclear weapons, time machine, and any other dangerous technology will be discussed by Congress. Don't you see, Barlow? These agreements won't have any validity. She will tell everybody that she was forced to this. Bring the media. They will be our witnesses.

This controversial being is supposed to bring peace. However, authorities are reluctant to follow his recommendations. While Barlow goes back to his base, Tony becomes part of the team disassembling the time machine. Mr. Graves is arriving with some foreign scientists.

Tony is visiting some educational centers upon their requests. His celebrity status has turned him into a local hero. While giving a pep talk to the next generation, he says, "Don't let Nikola's research languish in the darkness." Later, he meets the most intelligent child in the world. A professor tells Tony, "He's the reason we wanted you to come to our school. He's special. He's nine years old." Hey, fella. How did you get into an Ivy League university at your age? I don't know, they chose me. I am here giving lectures to people who are around the same age as my parents. What's your lecture about? It's about four-dimensional bodies. It's a complex topic for such a young man. Are you proud of being super smart? That's meaningless to me. Don't be smug. I have to tell you something, Doc. What's that? Our universe was destroyed ten years ago. That's impossible. Where are we then? We are in a parallel universe. The experiments with the time machine created more destruction than what they actually realized. Why did you say that? They created a disruption in the fabric of space-time that sent us through a wormhole into a different dimension. Where did you get that information? I did my own calculations. Take it and see it for yourself. This is mind-blowing! How can a young boy do this? Listen, he's a prodigy. We would appreciate it if you could take him under your wing. He may be a great addition to your staff. He's not doing anything in school, simply embarrassing classmates and teachers. He knows everything we can teach him and more. His IQ is close to 300. Nevertheless, his intelligence cannot save him from being socially clumsy. He struggles to fit in with people around him that do not understand him. He's the smartest student I've ever had. What about his parents? He's the son of two intelligent doctors. They are grateful to have a gifted son. He was encouraged to learn whatever he was interested in from an early age. They didn't impose any subjects. This precious kid is a polyglot. How many languages do you speak, Logan? I speak Armenian, English, French, German, Hebrew, Italian, Russian, Spanish, and Turkish. I may know a little bit of other languages by listening to people, I grasp the basics. That's stunning! I almost forgot that I have even invented my own language. What for? I created it to write poetry and novels, all out of curiosity. Aren't you afraid that people wouldn't understand it? No, not at all. What have you done to prove your knowledge? I created a free energy generator using renewable sources. The school principal approached Tony. He told him, "Logan is the reincarnation of the genius of lightning." You've got to be kidding. No, I am not. He's controversial, which has earned him some haters. He once said, "The divine is not who. It is what. A form of energy that creates everything. It's everywhere and nowhere at the same time." Imagine the reaction of religious leaders. That was preposterous! How do you reduce divinity to quantum energy? Logan smirked. It's within us and flows through us, and it is ourselves too.

After a while, Tony gathered himself to enquire Logan, "How exactly was our world destroyed?" The destruction of the ship created a vibration that reached a high frequency that expelled our planet into a mirror universe. Wait a minute, Logan. What's a mirror universe? It's the closest universe to ours among the multiverse. Is it the same? No, it has some almost imperceptible differences. What happened then? Both worlds merged into an advanced one. That sounds a little far-fetched. Time flux is a wave. I know that. Don't you consider that particles merging would produce some explosions? I haven't thought of it. How did you get to that conclusion? I had a dream in which it was revealed to me. You may have confused the image. Instead of a merge, you were witnessing a transit, with a blurry, sort of distorted image with a retrograde look until our planet finally stabilized in the recent created universe. That sounds probable. Do you believe the rest of my story? I need to analyze your data to verify the information for the date on which you told us that it took place. That's amazing. You are going to confirm my theory. How are you so sure? I am always right. Not always. You were wrong regarding the fusion of the two worlds. Nobody is perfect.

Government authorities won't recognize the destruction of the world due to the time machine operation. It is beyond doubt. As far as I am concerned, the machine could create tiny black holes that wouldn't be enough to suction our entire planet. It is happening at the quantum level. Do you understand, Logan? I guess. You are smart. However, you need to learn basic concepts of science to grasp the meaning of your visions. I also have lucid dreams. What? Yes, similarly to yours. They are vivid images of chaos and creation. You're the first person who understood my gift. We are both gifted. Some people say that I am the reborn Nicola. No, you are not. How are you so sure, Tony? Because I can see through his eyes.

There are some inconsistencies in your arguments. I will be back to you. Please don't leave me behind with all these kids. This is an ordeal for me. I promise you that I will contact you soon.

Tony told Alina about the supposedly reborn Nikola. Did you believe his story? At times, I did. However, there are some inaccuracies in his theory. He may have learned many of those things by watching videos online or reading some science fiction blogs. Don't you give some credit to the child? Yes, I do. He looks genuinely interested and knowledgeable about some topics that merely an old soul would. We should invite him and his parents for lunch over the weekend. Yes, that's a fantastic suggestion. If Barlow could join us, he would help us verify his assumptions. What about including Mr. Graves and Leon? At first, Mr. Graves was our adversary. Although with the passage of time, we became close friends. I should invite him. Regarding Leon, I don't know if he could be of any help. Remember that the organization has always been on our side. You are right.

Logan and his parents arrived at Tony's place. Barlow was next. Then Leon showed up. We're missing Mr. Graves. Is he coming after all? I guess he is. There's no reason he shouldn't come to share some time with all of his friends. The bell rang. That must be him. Yes, indeed. They started talking about science and life. What is your ideal life, Logan? To me, a perfect life is one isolated from society. Since I suffer from enochlophobia, I avoid being in crowded places. You're as eccentric as other geniuses. Barlow removed his hoodie to show his real self. Logan was flabbergasted. You aren't human. That's obvious. Where are you from? He's a Martian, Mr. Graves added. No, I am not. I am from interstellar space, a place no human has even glimpsed. This is Logan. I told you all about him. Do you know what entanglement means? Quantum entanglement is inexplicable. You are a smart cookie. What is the relationship between life and quantum mechanics? We know that life expresses itself through a quantum field of cosmic consciousness in space-time. You've given a great response.

Did you hear the news? No, what news? Government scientists have accomplished the quantum entanglement of living organisms. Which ones? Tardigrades. What? Yes, those eight-legged micro-animals. Why them? They are the most resilient animals that we know of. How did they achieve the spooky action from a distance? This phenomenon occurs when two subatomic particles get together to reflect each other's changes. They become mirror images of the same entity. It doesn't matter the distance. They took it to another level, from the subatomic realm to the animal world. What was the ultimate goal of such an experiment? Casper has been pushing for a more advanced time machine. He doesn't learn from previous mistakes. No, he doesn't. He's stubborn.

Scientists triggered this effect in blocks of atoms, more precisely, biological matter, by taking them to extreme freezing temperatures. The tardigrades were placed on a superconductor, forming the third state of qubits, the qutrits, increasing the performance of the quantum computer used to process the coding information with reliability. The first change they noticed was that the tardigrades altered their frequency. This was simply digitizing the tardigrades, wasn't it? Yes, it was. Changing the resonance frequency of the qutrits produced a change in the bodies of the tardigrades, which are basically water. This was a dielectric effect rather than quantum entanglement per se. Why do you say that? It was all staged to produce an expected result. What was the result of the experiment? They claim they were successful. However, most of the tardigrades died. That was foreseen.

If you believe everything they tell you, then you are a fool, Leon. They are holding vital information about the experiment. Yes, that's true. Do you think that you are not omnipresent, Logan? We are all. What about omniscient? I know where you are taking me. Are humans omnipotent? Theoretically, we are. Are you delusional, Doc? If you believe that you are different from that which you call the universe, your core, luck, nature, or the divine, then you are living a lie. We were created in his image and likeness. I see you are religious, Mr. Graves. I respect that. Logan doesn't have the same point of view. What's yours, young boy? I think that we are all energy, frequency, and vibration. Yes, he explained that to me in a previous conversation.

Throughout the universe, in a cosmic ocean, we travel to get to the deepest parts of it. The difficulty of reaching other worlds gets cranked up exponentially. The quantum search is incredibly complex. It challenges us in every aspect, taking our sanity to the edge. What happens if we zoom into this tiny world? If we zoom in on muons, past them, and leptons, we plunge deeper into the quantum-verse. At this level, things are basically the same. However, it is tough for us to distinguish one thing from the other. This is a quantum ocean of similar subatomic particles with odd behavior. This is a primordial soup of gooey submolecules. Is it finite or infinite? It is still a guess. It turns out that quantum computing, with its recent time crystal breakthrough, is bringing about the futuristic, super optimistic creation of a working space warp drive. Barlow interrupted, "That's not a thing of the future. Our civilization has it."

What do black holes let out? Black holes emanate a specific kind of quantum pressure. What for? They exert a quantum pressure, which leads to the multiverse. If we can explain where the pressure comes from, then it would be a blow back to the white holes. This recently discovered quantum nature of black holes adds this strange behavior to these monsters. Black holes are stranger than anything in the cosmos.

What do you know about doppelganger universes, or perhaps parallel universes? I'd rather call them mirror universes. Why? They are in the proximity of another universe, mirror images, with slight differences. I'd prefer to call them "daughter universes." Why? Logan asked. They are the birth of a mature universe. Whether we are squishy mortal meatballs or deities, what's our role in the universe? We have to take our civilization to higher stages. By the way, Logan will start as a trainee at our lab. That's going to be an amazing experience for him. Absolutely! Nikola approves of his inclusion. Why did you say that? As I've told you before, our minds are one.

Project Time Plus is the most recent attempt by the government to fix previous failures. The government believes it is entitled to establish eugenics since this is a harsh time that requires the survival of the fittest to get rid of the weakest or less desirable strains. What are they doing to go ahead with this madness? They are using hard-core criminals as guinea pigs for the experiments. Tony wants to stop this crazy idea. If we don't do that now, they will continue with the elderly and so on, until they get to us. Different organizations are planning to block the entrance to the labs. Casper is marketing the project as a recent discovery to make the nation more powerful to fight against belligerent adversaries. He explicitly stated, "This is not a ballroom. We are creating the weapons we need for the near future to protect our nation. We'll do whatever it takes to accomplish our goals." This is deepening the political turmoil. It fused the rage of political opponents and agitated the masses.

Radiation is another issue they are dealing with. The mysterious weapon was no longer a secret. People are aching, suffering the effects of this waste, creating a fear of death, making it the most pressing matter for people around the labs. Authorities were willing to advance despite the efforts displayed by organizations defending people's rights to an environment free of toxic chemicals. It was inconceivable that silence would allow the continuation of such criminal actions. The government, in response to protests, formulated a policy of reducing radiation emissions and controlling access to the labs.

Logan sat on a bench, awaiting instructions from the scientists on what to do on his first day. As soon as Tony saw him, he called his name out. Come on! He ran as fast as he could. We're going to a secret place underground. What are you doing there? We are creating a quantum beam. Logan says, "It's jaw-dropping." His eyes were popping out. He couldn't believe his ears either. He is in awe thereafter. He's curious, asking questions and seeking information about the research. This is a dream come true. Thank you for saving me from school. You have cosmic intuition, Logan.

Loose quarks are the main actors in this esoteric oddity. They are the core of matter. Nikola tells them, "I didn't get to distinguish quarks from gluons." Master! Logan is stunned. Now we have the chance to elaborate on sound research. Yes, complete my work, my friends.

Casper was fired as the government started making changes, including to their policies. Those evil experiments were canceled. They informed that those individuals involved are going to be prosecuted.

Tony's integrity is part of his reputation. The incoming authorities invited him to join the

95

revamped council of science. Even though he's busy with his current research, he accepted such a nomination. It is a privilege.

A disintegrator beam is in the works. The government is committed to developing this weapon as a cooperative effort among different nations, providing their best scientists. The motivation for such a device has been the alien presence, which has influenced their decision to use more weapons in recent years. It was about time for us to take a step toward a better defense system. We shouldn't be vulnerable to external forces with unknown purposes. It is our mission to get the most brilliant minds working together to create the necessary devices to face this alien threat. We need to get them involved in the security of our world.

Logan had a dream from which he scribbled the blueprint for a cutting-edge invention. In spite of that, in secret, other old state-of-the-art inventions are going to be developed. Why such old-state-of-the-art inventions? They were designed by Nikola. However, they never came off the drawing board. You should learn some useful techniques that have been beneficial to us. I am open to advanced ideas. When the time is right, you should learn how to breathe correctly, meditate, and use some advanced methods, such as Reiki. Enthusiasm was on Logan's face. He was happy with his recent position as a child scientist. Being at the lab provides him with a unique opportunity to develop his abilities as well as learn from the outstanding staff.

The process against Casper, Derek, Mr. Graves, and some former government officials has begun.

Tony says, "It is unfortunate he got involved in this horrific case." He should have known better. Leon is representing Pro Science, following up on the trial. Impunity is not an option. They can abide by the fifth amendment to refuse to cooperate with the Department of Justice to protect other authorities. They should cooperate, otherwise they are going to receive severe punishment. They may be protected by an executive order. The president can grant pardons to them under the Espionage Act and Selective Service Act. If they are convicted, the president can give them executive clemency. The commutation of their sentences would be an atrocity after all the harm they have caused to our world. The former allies are under siege now.

Logan is mentally constructing his designs. He meticulously chooses the size and materials and estimates the time frame to manufacture them. A mind machine that could store our thoughts in the form of qutrits. It is a sublime quantum computer, a dazzling sensation. I am receiving help from them. Thanks to his brilliant idea, error-free silicon-based computing will be possible. Where's Tony? We haven't heard from him in a couple of days. Something must have happened to him. I'm afraid that you are right. What happened, sir? We have a report that Alina and Tony were on the plain that crashed a couple of days ago. Where was that? It was in Strasburg. We didn't know they were on a trip. That's all I know. Did you retrieve the corpses? No, not yet. The authorities are looking at the wreckage area. It's going to take some time to identify the bodies. So far, we have the list of passengers provided by the airline. Moreover, we're going to cross the list with the airport boarding system. I'll get back to you as soon as we have news regarding those passengers. Logan tells the scientists, "They are still alive. I can feel it." Didn't you hear what he said? I did. However, there must be a mistake.

From above, Nikola, Barlow, Tony, and Alina were observing Earth. How does it feel to be at the top of the world? This first-hand experience is unbelievable. Our planet is a fragile, tiny spot floating in space, hanging there by gravity, coming from nowhere. Everything is awesome from up here. When I look back there, I see things clearly. There are no actual borders. No, my friend. We build frontiers with our minds and ambition. Conflicts divide countries. Even rivers flow from one country to the other without any physical restraint. Do you think that we will suffer the overview effect? What's that? The feeling of helping others, becoming a philanthropist, and engaging in global issues. Alina and I are activists. Thus, that's nothing advanced to us. We work to safeguard our environment, nature, wild life, and, believe it or not, humankind.

The defense appealed the decision of the court. They are going to request a retrial based on grounds of mistrial. The judge was partial since all the information was in the media.

A short circuit at the lab triggered a fire. Logan and the rest of the staff were rescued. Some of them inhaled smoke and have breathing problems. They are at the hospital at the moment. Authorities confirmed that Alina and Tony canceled their reservations at the last minute and they were not on the plane at the moment of the crash. When Logan got the news, he felt relieved that his friends were still alive. However, they didn't know their whereabouts. He was released since he didn't suffer any injuries during the fire. He's going back home with his parents. Are you okay, Logan? Yes, I am. However, I miss Tony and Alina. They are nice people. Tomorrow will be another day.

Nikola returns to the cosmos' collective consciousness. Barlow is on his way to another universe in search of some unique material, which is as scarce as common sense on our planet. What material is that, Tony? It's quanphene. I've never heard of it. Neither have I. It exists exclusively in the quantum-verse. We are here, far from solid ground, looking back at our home, spinning in the darkness of the vast space. Don't you think it's time to go back? Yes, indeed.

Logan, it's time to make your visualizations come true. Draw them, list the settings, and whatever comes to your mind. Don't leave anything to chance. They will assist you at every step. Logan says, "This lab is my stomping grounds."

Government projects are stalled. We need a brilliant mind to guide our scientists. Any country could have brought that person capable of catalyzing inventions to the next level. Bring Tony and his team. Do you think he will want to join us? Don't enquire him.

Alina gets to her office early in the morning. She writes an article for her blog, "Quanphene, the Next Element." As soon as she posted the article, she received many calls and messages arrived in her inbox by the thousands. This is an avalanche. I didn't know this was going to appeal to people. Most of them are scientists and journalists. The receptionist tells her, "Some government agents are looking for you." Again! What do they want? They want to talk to you. Did they tell you what the matter was? It's regarding your article on the blog. Tell them to come in. Alright. Hello! Save all the formalities. We are concerned that you have published an article regarding a national security matter. What does the material have to do with national security? You see, your short-sightedness. You don't see the implications of providing cutting-edge technology information to people who cannot understand it? However, there are foreign governments that are eager to get it in their hands for not-so-benevolent purposes. What should I do? You should come with us. What for? You should tell us everything that you know. Tony opens the door. I am afraid you won't take her anywhere. She needs to come with us to answer some questions. Call the legal department of the company. Her lawyer was standing at the reception by the time she called him. Gentlemen, first of all, who are you? We are government agents. Do you have any identification? We don't have to do that, sir. I'm afraid that you should leave then. I can tell you that I work for the alien control office. You both have to go to the MILL tomorrow. The president will be waiting for both of you. You can save the lawyer by now. Who were those clowns? They were sent by some agency. That's for sure. Do you know what the MILL is? I guess it is a secret task.

It would be fascinating to know what Nikola's thinking about this invention was. International scientists are hoping to receive extra help to decipher some of the pages of the manuscript. When Tony was introduced to the group, they were happy to see him. They wanted to show him their progress. He said, "What you have built here is a toy, gentlemen." We definitely need help to improve this device. We are sure that with your expertise, we can make significant improvements. It seems that you didn't understand me. This contraption is not workable. We have to go back to square one. Any misinterpretation of the instructions could have led you to this erroneous outcome. Can you understand Nikola's penmanship? Yes, of course. I see exactly what's in there. That's fabulous. Now we are moving in the right direction.

Logan is telling the team of scientists how he envisions artificial gravity to equip spacecraft with a suitable environment for humans. This effort is a non-governmental attempt to develop artificial gravity. First and foremost, we need to determine the energy required for such an endeavor. It's going to be based on anti-gravity, using quantum fields.

Alina is posting her most recent article on her blog about the fact that Casper and Derek received back-to-back life sentences, while Mr. Graves barely avoided consecutive life sentences. Even though they appealed, there's a slight chance for them to get reduced sentences.

Logan is finishing his quantum computer. The first test to wirelessly transmit intelligence is about to take place. This is an ancient aspiration of humankind. It is going to be possible today. Who's your volunteer? I will do it myself. Logan is going to transmit his intelligence to the computer. A reverberation was heard all over the town. It was reported to the emergency line. People were scared. They didn't know what was causing it. I didn't expect such a noise to be a side product of the transfer. We still have to improve in that aspect. Regarding the outcome, it was fantastically transmitted and recorded in the form of memory using 2.5 qutrits. Logan was notified that the quantum computer's crystal processor suffered from overheating. It could be fixed by improving the cooling elements. Anyway, this test provided enough data to imply its limitless applications.

Tony is visiting his private lab. How are things going without me? They are fine. We are complying with deadlines. Logan has almost finished the quantum computer. Tony was given insights into the intelligence transmission by the lead scientist. Thanks for the input. I will give Logan a piece of advice for future tests. The next stage of the development must be planned ahead to avoid any issues. Let me know well in advance when you are planning to have the next test. Of course, you should first correct all the loose ends to get better results. I will.

A scientist working for the MILL project detected a radio wave pattern that was unusual. What could have been this? It was a wave length that went through the quantum level. It seems to be voices in a movie. I'd rather say that they are memories transmitted through the air. Where to? That's an excellent question. Who may have been experimenting with this advanced technology? You should ask Tony that question. We can do better the next time. Track the signal and let us know. That sounds reasonable.

Our brains turn into waves transmitted at a specific frequency. That intelligence contains data that can be gathered by a recipient, the quantum computer, that decodes the waves and turns them into memory that is stored in the form of qutrits. It sounds simple, doesn't it? You've got to be kidding.

You didn't bring me down. You made it! Nikola says, "I will send my intelligence to be part of the universal database." I will be glad to receive it and store it for future generations. You all should do the same. Where are you going with this, master? As per consciousness, the cosmos' collective intelligence is unprecedented. Wouldn't it lead to artificial intelligence taking over humankind? If you let your fears control you, then you are doomed to fail. We are on the brink of a post-modern era cosmos.

Tony is motivating Logan to develop particularly stable and efficient quantum computing, thus speeding his calculations without losing his information quickly. Data has to be retrievable at any time. Unfortunately, in his most recent attempt, a couple of qubits lost their information rapidly. Don't get disappointed, Logan. You have to create a backup system with extra qubits to correct any errors due to its odd behavior. We are talking about millions of qubits. Let's talk about qutrits, then. A 3-level quantum system! Yes, it will prevent any loss of information. In addition, I'm working on a slim prototype. Don't use nanowires. I prefer a wireless connection. Use the simulator to see how they behave with such settings. Indium is excellent for semiconductors. Our lab uses advanced spectroscopic methods to choose the best materials.

When I see Logan, Nikola's inner voice comes to my mind. He says, "Don't let Logan get wasted." Why is that? He's extremely talented. However, he's fighting recurrent thoughts of quitting. He'd prefer to take a menial job than be a renown scientist. He's reclusive. He doesn't want others to know of his brainpower. He can do many exceptional things that will be relevant to the cosmos. He's trying to avoid higher expectations. He needs help to develop his EQ. I agree with you, master. Emotional intelligence is essential in our lives. At least once or twice during your lifetime, you will experience such an existential crisis. You have to be up to mutability and get away from ambiguity; no dichotomy at all. Have you asked Logan about his greatest childhood joy? No, I haven't. Why? I hadn't thought of that. You should. That way, you can get closer. He lacks friendship. You can create that sense of companionship, of being part of a team, or of a family. As astounding as it may sound, we live for one another. Cooperation is a vital part of our survival and progress. We thrive together since we are all in this together. Science is no different. I'm completely fascinated, master. You've given me the toolkit to get Logan on the right track and away from distractions. Bear in mind that sometimes we abandon ourselves, our wondrous and inventive minds drift apart. Journeys expand your vision of the world; you become more aware of your surroundings, more homesick, and more appreciative of what you have. Don't take things for granted. No, I won't. I was born during a thunderstorm. My life was not an easy one. I didn't expect it either.

People at the lab were startled by the work that Logan and Tony had put together. It is a masterpiece. We have offered the young man a scientific environment that is seldom seen at his age. This exposure is molding his character. I have no doubt that he will continue our steps. You'd better learn those steps from the masters. Logan is thankful that he is allowed to let his imagination wander. Tony tells him, "The government withheld information regarding Nikola." Why? A great idea that he wrote is powerful enough to be scary. Even today, it is inconceivable. What is that? I'm glad that it sparked your curiosity. I pledge not to tell anybody. I know you won't. He thoroughly describes a robotic army. What's more, he subtly implies that they could be self-replicating and self-repairing. That's insane. How do you link the robots to the time machine? I don't. The master of lightning did.

Sometimes in life, we act like robots, mechanically or automatically, reacting passively throughout our lives. Do you understand the importance of transmitting intelligence to the memory of a quantum computer? No, I don't fully understand it. I imagined that. Time will show you the potential of what you've done.

Logan nonetheless worked tirelessly to catch up with the adult scientists at the lab. Tony was observing his pace. A twister was created by the force field. The apparent simplicity of this advanced device was on the surface. In fact, it is a powerful and destructive force. Although usually quiet and subdued in public, Logan is more talkative when at the lab working with his fellow scientists. What are you working on, Logan? I am working on what the late professor called the "flaming sword." Ah, a laser weapon. You need to transform, transmit, and direct energy at will. How are you going to fuel the sword and control the intensity of the beam? Those are the key elements that I am addressing right now. We come to work every day to find solutions to problems such as the ones you are facing at the moment. That's right. What is your ultimate goal? What do you mean, Tony? Is it going to be a showmanship artifact or the real deal? I don't try to impress anybody. My goal is to have an efficient, powerful laser. What for? I don't know. That's the problem; you have a childish vision. It is neither a toy nor a magic trick. It is a weapon that can harm people. However, it could have other uses. What other uses? It could be used for cutting metal, wood, rock, or any other material. It would be similar to an advanced machete. What about a combo of machete, saw, and precision slicer? You are getting creative. I love that.

Tony is compelled to confront government authorities. He blatantly resigned from his position on the scientific committee. He doesn't want to be involved in any fight with alien visitors. That would result in a tough loss. Besides, the government has a hidden agenda that includes the potential development of the time machine. Now they call it a retrospective camera, referring to traveling into

106

the past. I am completely disgusted with how this project is being managed. Your ethics are tarnished by all your actions. He decided to give a speech at Congress explaining his current decision.

Leon and Pro Science members were arrested, and nobody has seen them since then. Alina is investigating what may have happened to them. I need to find out their whereabouts. At least I want to know that they are fine.

Nikola, floating in the air, came as a vision to Tony. I will speak for you. My words will flow through your tongue. This is an ill-fated adventure that may end up as a huge failure. However, I will take my chances. There's nothing left to lose for us. I'm too upset to accept the upward trend of disappearing people and controlling media.

Getting up at 5 a.m. Tony had slept for three hours. Nikola was using his hand to write each and every word. I'm guided by Nikola's hand. Foreseeing a turbulent future, he chooses the correct words to tell future generations how he behaved and what he did to protect humankind. I can't find the right words to express all the emotions that pass through my heart. Nevertheless, it is imperative that I depict the chaos you are causing in the world. As he wrote his words, he was in front of Congress, reading them out loud. The audience was mesmerized by the selection of words and how impeccably he was attired. On behalf of the late mastermind, Nikola, I would love to address you all today. It is at this time that we need to carefully assess the full effect of such an aggressive policy of creating mass destruction weapons to fight against advanced civilizations. I am vehemently opposed to using science for war. It is not a tool to accommodate a presidential run. Rather than rely on its scientific staff, schemes are being used to force scientists from other countries to participate in such obscure projects. One congressman said, "He's not human. He's an alien." That's the reason he's defending their interests, not ours. Arrest him!

Things were completely wrong for Tony. Alina is still searching for her friends. She got stuck in the middle of a protest requesting freedom for all the scientists that were illegally arrested. Some police officers were carried away by the protesters and they used tear gas, rubber bullets, and water cannons to disperse them. A shooting around the corner, followed by another. She was caught in crossfire. She fell in the middle of the street. Some of the protesters helped her. She was picked up by an ambulance and taken to the hospital. Alina's aunt visited Tony and gave him all the details. She's undergoing emergency surgery to extract some bullets. Tony's lawyer bailed him out. He rushed to the hospital to see Alina. I regret leaving her alone. However, I can't help it.

A swarm is approaching Earth. What's that? They may be comets. I doubt these are comets. The speed and maneuverability are unnatural. The astronomers warned the government. Scientists were gathered to discuss the possibilities. At the speed they are coming toward our planet, they will be here in no time. What do you mean? They are getting closer at a slow speed. They want us to see them. If they wanted to surprise us, they would have swooped down and that was it. Gentlemen, focus on the task at hand. What's your report? That's a fleet of alien spacecraft. They are coming after us.

Pro Science members continue to be targeted by police. Some raids have taken place in the last few days. However, it did not deter Tony's effort toward unmasking the government's massive destruction weapon projects. It has caught the attention of the general public.

Logan is trying to focus on one of his ideas at a time. I must keep my mind in the present. If I keep wandering into the future, I will not achieve any of my goals. He is accompanied by his mother to visit Alina at the hospital. At the ICU door, Tony was standing waiting for news regarding his beloved Alina. After they greeted him, they asked how things were. She has not improved since the surgery. A doctor comes walking rapidly and pushes the door. How's she? I'm sorry, sir. We did all we could. Her agony and pain are over. Half awakened, Tony is thumping around, smashing his fists against the wall. He's completely frustrated. Some journalists came over to interview him. One reporter asked him if he was going to file a lawsuit against the city or the police. I'm in too much grief to talk. My sweetheart. Everything's gone. They've destroyed my life. Life is fragile. It doesn't last long. We have to enjoy every moment we have together. In the end, all that matters most is how you lived your life. If you get to old age, all happiness comes from memories of the great old days.

Mr. Graves couldn't come to the funeral. He called Tony and said, "My deepest sympathy, my friend. She didn't deserve to end up this way."

Thank you for calling. I know that. Moreover, friends and colleagues expressed their condolences. The road to the graveyard took an eternity. The line of vehicles, flowers, and farewell to the love of your life. Things you never prepare for in life. You know that it may happen one day if you don't go first. However, you don't even want to think about that unfortunate event.

The following day, Tony was nostalgic, longing for the old days when they were together. Sinking in sorrow, he was melancholic. We all have bad days, my friend. Don't plunge into sadness. What else can I do? She was my guiding spirit. Nikola's words came to his mind, "Severe blistering of the soul, that's all a loss accounts for." He tries to keep himself busy. He goes to the lab. Things are hectic as usual. Then he talks to Alina's coworkers. They informed him that his friends from Pro Sciences were found dead on a supposedly derailed train. How many people were there? There were seven people. What about Leon? He couldn't make it. That's too sad. There are moments in life in which things get accumulated and an avalanche of bad news keeps hitting you. You have to move on with your life, that's what they say. It's tough. You learn to live with the pain. You never forget your beloved ones that were lost along the way.

Scientists are concerned about the alien visitors floating above our planet. What are they waiting for? They may be monitoring our actions. They came to deter governments from creating weapons that we don't have the faintest idea of how powerful they are. Everything we say is speculation. They are not moving. This is a serious problem. It would lead to the exhaustion of our energy. Why do you say that? They are almost covering the sun of a continent with their spacecraft. They are huge. Do you think that there are many beings in the spaceships, or are they giants? It's a herculean task to tell from here. Both are plausible since we don't know who we are dealing with. Skepticism has been our policy. What are we going to do this time? There's no way we can hide this invasion. It's more than obvious. Prudence should be our policy. Even amateur astronomers with a telescope can see them coming.

I should stop this senseless race for the ultimate weapon. How can I do that? Nikola would use diplomacy over anything else. I have been enthused over the results at our labs. I have to go back to work to get distracted from these remorseful thoughts. Logan spares some hope for the future.

One of the spaceships is descending. Where is it going? It's over the capital of the country. Is it landing? No, it isn't. It's hovering above, now it's going back to its previous position among the fleet. Most governments have activated the nuclear protocol. They are ready to launch a massive attack of missiles. That would cause more damage than any potential benefit. We may kill ourselves with the radiation that will cover our planet. That's pretty stupid.

Undaunted, the presidents' summit decides to impose a global emergency state, confinement, and curfews. That won't work since people are aware of the danger those alien invaders may carry to us. You are calling them "invaders" However, we don't know their real intentions. Simply look at all those spaceships. If it were a peace mission, they wouldn't come here with such a display of power. That's right.

In a spin so quick that even with high-speed cameras it has to be paused. The fleet took the plunge into our atmosphere and flew, barely skipping buildings. An attack was ordered. They are trespassing in our space without requesting it. The launching platforms all over the world were activated. The alien spacecraft had invisibility shields. Thus, they vanished in front of our eyes. Our radars were useless. All the missiles that were launched were frozen in mid-air. This is not reality. This is a paused video. What kind of magic is this? Whatever it is, it means we failed to keep up with their technology. I absolutely can't explain what's going on. There's a way we can detect them. What is that? It is odd that a child is telling us what to do. Put everything aside, guys. Tell us, Logan. Let's assume that it is an electromagnetic cloak. We need to use electromagnetic waves at different frequencies to diffuse the invisibility effect. Another way, if it is a quantum cloak, is to use a quantum beam of photons to create an entanglement. Get to work, guys. The first attempt was not successful. They are preparing the beam to shoot photons at high speed. Get ready, set, and shoot. It works. This boy is locked in, and he delivered. He's an unsung hero. Yes, he's committed to doing this. We have to be firmly fixed in our position. The sky above us is flickering, pixelated. We can see part of their fleet. This was an outstanding idea. They didn't expect that from us.

The attack was a flop. Even though the spaceships were located. We're just holding it. There's nothing to get hold of them. What can we do to stop them? Listen to that loud whistle. Most of the people exposed to the whistle fainted. Tony didn't, since he was isolated in a vacuum chamber. He has been monitoring everything that's happening on the surface of the planet. I knew they were going to use high-pitched frequencies to attack us.

Despite the recent issues with nuclear weapons, governments still think that they can fight against alien troops. How are we going to do that? Artillery, bullets, whatever we have at hand. Don't surrender. Not yet. There's still much we can do. At some point, we've got to make decisions that suit us for the long haul. Let's take our chances. Scientists reported to the authorities what they had a consensus about. We were protected by the quantum shield. We recommend you use the quantum beam at its maximum power. None of us have that weapon. We have Logan, the prodigy scientist. He has developed one. We shot at them with it to remove the invisibility cloak, and it worked perfectly. You have the green light to proceed. We are going to back you up with regular weaponry in case you need it. Thanks.

It soon becomes clear that whatever we do is going to be useless against this advanced civilization. They considered us so insignificant that they didn't even try to communicate with us. Tony is reaching out to the stars, contacting the cosmos' collective consciousness. He's meditating, entering a deep trance that would allow him to

113

astrally travel to the space where human and alien souls share a common place, the same fiber of space-time. They know the secrets of the universe. They can help us save our tiny blue planet.

Nobody is coming to help us. We'd better face our own fears. Don't be so tough on yourself. We are with you. Thanks for the support. However, there's nothing you can do in the material world. You are spiritual beings. You don't destroy or kill. We, humans, are the ones to fight against evil. You are wrong, Tony. We can manifest our spirits into your dimension. There's so much we can do to prevent any evil beings from harming your planet. Any help is welcome during these convulsive times. Anyway, we don't perceive any evil in those beings. Are you sure? Yes, I am.

Pursue your dreams, Logan. Never give up. No matter what others tell you. You are not the future of the world, you are the present. That's how desperate we are. Advance the world to a new era of prosperity and freedom.

Aliens removed nuclear components from our weapons. They didn't destroy anything. As soon as they finished their mission, they departed for the depths of the universe. Governments were evaluating the damages. Our weapons are useless. It will take years to get back to where we were before their invasion. That's what they wanted. What was that? They wanted to prevent us from using such weapons. Now I understand it. Thus, most leaders decided to expand their nuclear programs.

The day after the aliens left, Tony joined his master in the cosmos' collective consciousness. I

114

transcended my mortal existence. I will look after Logan to guide him through every challenge. Our visitors are in the vicinity. I can sense their benevolence. Aside from having a positive impact on the universe, they are also attempting to influence us in the right direction. I can see it clearly ten years in the future: annihilation on Earth. You will be killing each other with your new mass destruction weapons. Why? Power nonsense will devastate one another. These are going to be the most dangerous years in human history. You must build spaceships to escape from the last days on the planet. Nikola tells him, "You can astrally reach them. Tell them what to do." I still think that I can trust Logan. If you do that, then prepare him for the coming years. These events are unavoidable.

Logan wakes up from a dream. It was a nightmare. He was sweating even though he was in an acclimatized room. The images are frozen in my mind. "Operation Exodus" is our priority. I feel a presence. It must be Tony's. You don't have to convince anybody. Those committed to life who are against weapons are welcome. Whoever is belligerent should be left behind. Focus on the task at hand. What's that? You need to lead the operation and arrange all the logistics needed to evacuate the planet in less than ten years. That's not enough time. It is if you start right away.

This generation is different to any previous one. It is immersed in a technology-obsessed culture. Conquering the cosmos requires going beyond the local galaxy to enter interstellar territory. These endeavors will provide new planets for human settlements. Nikola never wanted to be a cult celebrity. The future is theirs. They have a challenge. It's a shortcoming as well, to overcome. They need to educate people. Ignorance is ruling the world with its conscious limitations. Science is our mother. It should be our supportive guide. Our energy will gear the universe in a way that will allow us to get past the uncharted territory, reaching for the hidden worlds where the strangest beings reside. This is going to be a turning point in the exploration of deep space. Enough of thinking about the future. We must devote all of our efforts to this uncertain present to build the foundation for the great future that awaits us.

Every nation has valuable people that start volunteering toward the goal of building spaceships. Millions have been signing up for the journey out of this planet. We cannot squander this unique opportunity to expand our horizons. We have to grow to be technologically advanced enough to reach the depths of space and spread our race over interstellar space. We're not going to hop from one planet to another. We must confirm the planets or moons that can harvest life. They should be suitable for human life. Traveling throughout the cosmos will indeed change our humanity. No human has ever stepped foot on any other planet. The only other place humankind has been is our companion moon. That's soon to change. There are trillions of planets as possible destinations. They are too far from us. Nikola surely has an answer to the biggest question. I should ask him. How are we going to those distant planets? You don't need faster than the speed of light spaceships or teleportation devices. You neither have to get antimatter engines nor anti-gravity propulsion. It's going to be through portals. Earth is surrounded by plenty of portals to other dimensions. Are those the shortcuts we are looking for to make possible interstellar travel? There are ancient portals that were created for an exclusive reason. They are waiting for us to discover them. All we have to do is adventure into the unknown.

Logan talks to the world assembly. Since it is highly unlikely that we will find a planet similar to Earth, it is best if we begin our transit to other worlds by terraforming those planets in our vicinity. In a matter of a few years, we can have other places where we can start human settlements. That sounds plausible. From there, we can move to other neighboring systems that have habitable planets. Our legacy for future generations would be to make space accessible to humankind. What about a man-made planet? That's still far-fetched. Although I'm sure that we will learn how to create them along the way, it is imperative that we find other solutions in the short-term.

Many people want to escape an overpopulated world with overcrowded cities. They are suffering greatly as a result of the energy crisis. Water wars are the most common threat to peace. Pollution is all over the world and, in conjunction with global warming, is making the Earth a hostile place to live in. The old planet has reached its limits of sustainability for human life. It is time to leave it behind.

Nikola sees himself in the dark. The world left him alone, bouncing from one hotel to another. He was living in small hotel rooms since his debt was huge and he didn't have the money to pay it. The hype and hoopla around his inventions has vanished. Although he felt weak, he crossed the street several times to feed his beloved pigeons at the park. One cab was coming toward him at high speed, and the driver swerved to avoid him. However, he couldn't. Nicola couldn't dodge it either. He was thrown onto the asphalt. He was taken to the hospital. When reporters asked about his condition, his doctor said, "He is in stable condition. However, his back was severely bent and three of his ribs were broken." Tony was awakened by a vision. What happened? I was there. At the moment when Nikola had the accident. Now I can see more. He was released from the hospital. Nevertheless, he never sought medical help after the accident. His injuries and wounds were untreated and he never fully recovered from the accident. That was a lifelong custom, even though this time he was going to pay the toll for his stubbornness. His remains were cremated. An urn with his ashes was taken back to his country. Even though he was not religious, a dispute took place over his remains: whether to rebury them in the orthodox church or keep them at his museum.

Science's ultimate goal is to improve humankind. I always knew the invisible world was inches away. People say that I'm a visionary, sort of a mystic man. I am more sensitive and connected to all realms. Although some may believe that my scientific work has nothing to do with paranormal phenomena, it is true that the unknown has always been a part of my life. Psychic experiences were not made public to avoid any association with occultism or spiritualism. I was sure that there was more than energy and matter. Vibrations and frequencies brought me the sense of something else. Many extrasensory episodes were provoked by this habit I had of being a recipient of communications, sort of a medium, to communicate with beings in other dimensions. That, in time, developed my intuition. I once experienced a vision of a cloud full of angels with a lovely and motherly perception. I stared at the cloud. Then I saw my mother, and later, a choir of heavenly voices, singing an indescribably beautiful song. Another similar event happened when his sister's image appeared and disappeared. Angeline had a close call. Through the cosmos' collective souls, I got the link to Tony, whom I guided through the perils of convulsive times. My legacy was at stake. Our partnership, this spiritual bond, provided me the opportunity to redeem my inventions, save them from being lost in the darkness.

Logan, wake up! Who are you speaking with? Myself. Where am I? You are at the lab. What happened? I saw Nikola and then Tony. I can see what they both saw. It's time we begin the search for the portals. How are we going to do that? We are going to do that by using electromagnetic waves from towers. How many towers do we require? Not many. We are going to use ground conductivity. The master's dream is going to come true. Our old faithful will have rings like Saturn. Those rings will signal the places where the portals are located.

The primary goal of the tower is to provide wireless electricity. We must develop a global wireless system to cover our entire planet. What kind of waves does it use? It uses air-borne electromagnetic waves. It can travel through the ground and back to the air. Nikola's design can be improved by adding upper layers for a more efficient, conducive way of generating electricity. The world will glow. What about using geothermal energy from the core of our planet? This is an enormous operation. We need to get hold of any possible source to feed the towers that will distribute electricity without any ripples of disturbance throughout the whole globe, spreading it freely. Wireless power transmission eliminates the need for wiring.

Do we have enough funds to cover the cost of this project? All the nations that are cooperating altogether are providing exactly what we need, all the materials and equipment. Besides the gear needed for the operation, everything is going to be transmitted through the ground and the air. Thus, no extra cost is added. That's true. As we advanced towards the construction of the towers, some alien spacecraft were seen above the site. What are they monitoring? Our construction, of course. If they assisted us, that would make a great difference. We received some donations. What are those? These are electric towers that were used in the fields of the countryside. The team working at Tony's lab manufactured the cupola for the top of the tower. It has violet lights on it.

Some government officials came to see Logan. Is there anything I can do for you, gentlemen? Yes, sir. You are a grown-up now. Have we met before? Yes, we have. We met you when you were just a child working on your internship at the lab. I see you have a good memory. You are leading the post-Nikola era. We brought you a gift. What's that? This is a blueprint of Nikola's underground sites. Some are supposedly considered to be portals to other dimensions. Thanks for this valuable piece of history. Although we cannot guarantee what it promises, it's all up to you to find them. We're going to use it on behalf of our fellow Earthlings.

A dream ahead of our time. We have embarked on the most ambitious plan of colonizing other planets in a short-term period. Nikola's voice is becoming familiar to me. I hear that voice like my inner voice. He says, "You're not just powering the world. This is also a powerful communication system." How does it work? You have to find the right frequencies. 369, at 432 Hz. That is an ancient frequency that has been linked with healing properties. This magic frequency will revolutionize the world. A vibrational healing device? Yes, it is music with sub-bass pulsation. Your subconscious mind's journey through space with these waves is going to unveil hidden powers. This particular frequency has a direct effect on structures, people, and the surroundings. We'll reprogram people's minds through this frequency. For the first time in history, people are listening to what we, as scientists, have to say about the future of our planet and the universe. Since it has to do with avoiding the extinction of humankind, I hope they take action. You can feel the atmosphere of excitement rather than sadness. Some of us will be departing for a new world, leaving our beloved planet Earth behind. Even though it is foreboding, Nikola's device is first unveiled. A passage to other dimensions where the secret frequencies are first heard without mutes. They are meant to describe the magnificence of sounds in a dazzling symphony that harmonically creates this concerto of life. Then you will listen to the recurring rhythms that invoke the type of communication that Tesla's tower may have transmitted. Multiple rhythms are overlapped with an increasing intensity. As the complexity reaches its peak, sounds are stacked to their zenith, playing a harmonious melody that announces the coming of a new era. It has a subliminal message in its beats. One rhythm that occurs repeatedly throughout the sonata in different modes, spells out the last name of the master: "T-E-S-L-A," and it is a masterpiece that mesmerizes everybody.

 Nikola was always considered to be straightforward. I don't think he was a cynic. On the contrary, he was a truthteller, excessively honest, and he did everything for the sake of science, not for money. He ended up living his life in poverty. Nikola and Tony are my role models. This wireless electricity project was a magnificent idea. However, in less than a year, it went awry and ended up sinking Nikola scientifically and economically. It won't happen to me. This time I have enough support to accomplish this goal.

Logan began the global transmission of wireless electricity, along with the melodic sounds at the right frequency. This experiment will take us to unexplored territory. Nikola knew that high frequencies had many advantages and applications. Now we can see that lamps are glowing brighter worldwide. This is smooth. Energy is transmitted efficiently. What's more, it is less dangerous than using wires. It passes harmlessly through your body. Nikola was fixed to the frequency of the sun, a cycle of five minutes, which is 0.033 hertz. The number 3 is present in it. The sound bounces back from deep into the sun. These sounds are disturbances in pressure that travel away from the source. The sun has many beautiful harmonics. Each vibrates at a different frequency. The sun's resonance is inaudible to us since it is too low for us to hear.

People around the world are enjoying this sonata. This is art. I could spend the whole day listening to it. It is aesthetically intriguing. Where does it come from? It may be from the sun or the core of our planet. Speculation is the order of the day. Logan tells his colleagues, "Timing couldn't have been better." Why? We were not embroiled in any other problems at the time. What about the flying saucers? I am not concerned about them. The government should. The aliens may come and give us a hand. With their expertise, we can accomplish our goals in no time.

There is news of electricity coming from the ground in great prairies, big cities and rings around the planet's equator. There are no wires. This is odd. In the evening, the sky was fully lit, and some scientists even said, "It could light the vacuum of space." The resonant frequency produced an enthusiasm never seen before. Logan and his team were going to use the frequency of space as a bonus. The frequency is in the range of 8 hertz. Another change was going to be introduced. We need to transmit electricity eighty kilometers above the atmosphere, in a region called the ionosphere, where Nikola once said that it was the most conducive area of the planet. We have a problem, Logan. What's that? How are we going to send electrical power to that altitude? While they were thinking of ways to perform their task, they picked up a signal. This is stunning. We don't have time for this overwhelming phenomenon. What are we going to do regarding the signal? It is from outer space. I'm sure that those beings are trying to communicate with us to help us. What if they were just trying to prevent us from embarking on our interstellar endeavor? I am not going to assume anything. Let's contact them right away.

When people received the information that aliens were contacting us, this time nobody ridiculed us. Logan has a brilliant idea that he inherited from the fruitful mind of his master. They paused for the rest of the day. However, they will continue in the morning with more power and a secret device to get into the ionosphere.

When the morning comes, Logan is still there, staring at the sky. A particle beam, that's it. This idea arouses curiosity and interest among the scientific community. Some feared that if he succeeded, he would create a black hole that would destroy our planet. I made sure that the technical description was clear enough that even political leaders would understand it. No more conjectures. The day has come with a new opportunity to achieve the impossible.

It's troubling to think about the millions of frequencies that pass through our bodies every second, similarly to particles. It is absolutely unbelievable that they are perpetually around us. Some may be kind of obnoxious, though. If we understood frequencies better, we could cope with vibrations in a broad way. We live in a broad band of frequencies. Visible light is the only frequency band that we can see in the spectrum, which is a meaningless fraction of the infinitesimal amount of existing matter in the universe that is perceived by our senses or our limited equipment. Logan! Logan! What happened? You're drifting. Stop daydreaming. We've got to finish this. Where are we sucking up all this energy? It comes from diverse sources, mainly by harnessing geothermal spots as well as the sun.

We are going back to our origins, to our source, to be like our creator. That's our purpose. We are children of the cosmos. We'll be back to it. We come from cosmic dust, and one day we'll be back in that dust. Nikola reminded Logan not to forget to write down his ideas. Right after a lucid dream, write them down. Don't leave anything to your memory. Despite how they sound. It is not awkward to imply that they are out of this world, don't doubt them. They came to you for a reason. The future always tells the truth about your ideas. Develop them in order to accomplish your inventions.

Force and matter, reason and no-reason. The accommodating Earth will soon be no longer home for us. Our starships are almost ready to take a detour to our destination. We no longer need warp speed. However, there are minimum standards required for humans to adapt to the space environment. Precautions regarding gravity, radiation, oxygen, pressure, and temperature are still considered the most important settings for humans to embark on space trips. It is required to have a closed-loop life support system for humans that will keep us alive through the portal and beyond. What will happen to those we leave behind? They may construct underground shelters. Anyway, not many would survive under such conditions.

Logan made contact with the alien visitors. They wanted to make sure we didn't destroy the planet. I told them, "We are escaping an inevitable end." How come? They are unreasonable people who will place power over reason and force over matter. Although we have sped up the search for planets that can sustain human life, it would be great if you could assist us with your expertise. We've been observing you up close, trying to understand you. You are weird creatures. Why do you say that? Humans destroy everything, including their own lives. That's true. Our level of civilization is low, and our leaders are blinded by power and control. We asked ourselves how we could help these thriving beings overcome their own misery. The best answer is to provide you with some information about the path you have taken, diverting from the right track. How can we return to the road of progress and evolution? That's a question you have to answer for yourself. As an outsider, all I can tell you is that your choices have been poor. The worst thing to do is destroy your only planet. What were you thinking of? It's outrageous to see how incompetent we have been, not to see the irreversible damage we have done to nature. It is beyond what you see. Whatever you harm in your world affects us. This is an intertwined cosmos. Even our souls are linked to a bigger structure. Correct me if I'm wrong, but you are talking about the superstructure of the cosmos, which we call the cosmos' collective souls. We may be talking about the same thing. However, your understanding seems to be limited. Ascension and transcendence are meaningless to you. You become attached to material things that you will have to abandon. You came to this land naked, and you are going back to the cosmic dust empty-handed. I know that. If you noticed, most of us are scientists or people who want to live in a more developed civilization. Chaos is a matter of barbarians. We don't want to be part of that. I see that not everything is lost. There's still hope for your race. What about yours? What do you want to know? Where do you come from? We come from the depths of space, past the herculean barrier. What's your planet's name? It's home. We don't have such things as names. Is there any other civilization like yours? We are not the only ones in the universe. Don't spread the seeds of destruction to other planets in this universe. We have seen that many times before, with horrific results. We're going to do our best not to disappoint you. Anyway, are you going to help us on our quest? Your success or flops are not going to blur our view of how you have predated your own planet. Where should we start looking for another place we can call home again? We are quite sure that you have most of that already figured out. Aren't you going through one

127

of the portals? Yes, that's correct. However, we don't know which one could take us to the right location, a place where we can settle. You may then be exposed to errors, oversights, or miscalculations, and you could need a biodome or some other structure where you are going to. Why don't you send an exploratory mission first? We are desperately reaching out to you to get some suggestions. You are exposing yourself to unexpected harmful effects, lethal surprises, and undesired conditions. Are we bound to become at least a multi-planet civilization? It's all up to you. Some eventual calamity would make you extinct. Follow your guts; there are many worlds through any of the portals. You can choose whichever best suits your conditions and needs.

Our first manned interstellar voyage has begun, an exploratory mission led by Logan, Dana, and Ian. An odyssey nobody prepared for. There was also no time for rehearsing either. It's true that our journey was not pushed by any cataclysm. However, the tension and war that could erupt at any time certainly gave us the best motivation to flee a world that is hostile enough to a reasonable person. This journey will provide us with the information we need for a future exodus.

Two neighboring countries are in conflict for geopolitical reasons, including pipelines to reach Europe. An attack would be horrific for this small country. This confrontation could be avoided through the usual diplomacy channels. However, some leaders prefer the use of force over negotiations. Imposing your military power over a less fortunate country is disastrous. Logan was secluded in a mountain cabin for weeks before his adventure into interstellar space. His fellow scientists at the lab were worried that he may have lost his mind. He told some friends that he was in contact with aliens, like Nikola did. If he's following Tony and Nikola's steps, then we have to worry. Although he would have preferred to stay at the mountain, as a hermit, he returned to civilization to join the group on the exploration of uncharted areas of the cosmos.

Even though these nations deny any possible war, troops were deployed along their border. It is insane. You have to do what you preach. Unleashing such an army would definitely annihilate most of their population. Panic is taking over the general population. This could spark a global conflict, polarizing forces in two camps. Everyone defends his own interests. Logan thinks that we should designate a prison planet to send those who destroy and create chaos in our world. So far, we only have one planet. Due to our ambitions and interests, we do as we don't care for anything or anyone. What a selfish attitude. We don't have an escape spot. It's crazy how they escalate their rhetoric and threaten to use nuclear weapons as if they were on a distant planet. They don't measure the consequences of their actions.

Logan and his colleagues are approaching the ionosphere on their way to the portal. We are pushed by the rings of energy around our planet. As they enter the tunnel, they can see a vortex of energy around them. The spaceship is equipped to resist the turbulence of the portal. Are we going to the past or to the future? We'll soon find out about it. This is a magnetic portal that will close in a few minutes. How are we coming back? That's something we don't know yet. We are almost on the other side. Oh, no, no! What's wrong? We are on the other side of the sun. Behind the sun? That's correct. This is a stargate. We're too close. Let's correct our course. Wait a minute, Dana! This is not our sun. This is a red giant. There are three potential planets in the Goldilocks region. They started a round of flybys and ultimately decided to send a robotic rover to explore those worlds. It has special gear aboard. What's that? It has a drone that will speed up the process of exploration, taking samples and probably spotting where life may have flourished on the planets, if there's any around this system.

A successful mission that detected two great options and a potential third planet, in case of an emergency. The first planet is too hot. However, the poles still hold some water. A dome-like structure with acclimatized temperature is needed to inhabit it. The second choice is similar to Earth. It's bigger. Thus, its gravity force is stronger. Breathable air is available, and we noticed life in different spots. Intelligent life or artificial structures were not visible in plain sight. They may have their habitat underground. The third planet is too cold for humans. More research is needed to rule it out.

Look over there! Yes, I see another portal. Let's go through it. This is the fastest I've ever been in my entire life. Where will it take us? Another sun. This is ours. We're back. Another portal ahead. I can't avoid it. They went through it and arrived safely at... Where is this, guys? I don't know How is it possible? We were in outer space and, getting into this perturbation of space-time, we were suddenly brought back to Earth. Some military officers came to them. Where are we? This is Camp Hero. There's surely a connection between those points. How come? There are too many things we don't fully comprehend.

A meeting at the global assembly is taking place. Our heroes are back with valuable information. A tug of war begins among the delegates of different nations. They are afraid of us. Why is that? They know that we can think. We don't believe all of their lies. It's scary when you face lies with science. They always take advantage of your needs. Not in our case. That's not possible. We have what they don't have. What's that? We have privileged knowledge regarding new worlds, new options, and an escape plan. The secretary of the assembly starts the session with a warm welcome. This is a great moment in the history of humankind that provides us with an unequal opportunity to develop our potential.

Nikola astrally travels back home. They accomplished my dream of having rings around the planet. Wireless electricity for all! Present is theirs. Tony and Logan after him, two generations of men of science. What else can I ask for? I knew that traveling to outer space was a matter of time. Life is the motivator, not escaping conflict. It is true that invention is the engine that makes the world go around. However, there are discoveries that stun us, such as those portals to other dimensions. Logan meticulously tracked the signal of those alien messages. Besides, he figured out how to spot the portals without any help. He had my notes on electromagnetism that could lead to finding them.

We have substituted our lab for outer space. Theories were replaced by experiments. We all need theories to be proved. That's true. However, we discovered an entire cosmos through the portals. We crave novelty. This exceeded our expectations.

Nikola's in the park. There are new pigeons. I can't feed them like I used to do. People pass by my side. They can't see me. Only those with highly active perception can sense my presence. The pigeons do. They are happily flying around me. Everything is temporary, even life itself, including those individuals who were at the top of the world and the greatest scientists. We all have an expiration date on our genes. It is a death sentence. Logan asks telepathically, "What have you learned about the cosmos's collective souls? It is a community, our cosmos's collective soul community. We are part of the fabric of the universe. We feel the angst of those in fear because of an imminent war. Can you do something to prevent it? Our time was up long time ago. We are just the guardians of a legacy. The observers of a world that is blind to seeing beyond its nose. People whose arrogance controls them.

Nikola and Tony sat on a bench at the park. Logan comes to join them. Don't make our mistakes, Logan. What do you mean? You should not sacrifice your personal life for science. It is not worth it. The government is indifferent. You will receive no gratitude, no recognition in life. They will recognize you if you are loyal to their interests.

That's not what we are for. Let love come into your life. Instincts transcend your acumen. Trust your gut in moments of desperation. Feed the pigeons for me, please. He opens a canary seed bag. You see, they are grateful, they enjoy the food and they remember you.

Almost two million people have been displaced. Many will become refugees at the border of their neighbors. They are not doing anything to ease the tensions between these countries. Concerns have been reignited by the recent deployment of troops. An imminent nuclear attack has been ordered. The powerful eastern country wants to showcase to the world its weaponry and determination. They made an irrational decision instead of a levelheaded decision, that could have serious implications for global peace and the balance of power. Alexander, a submarine officer, refused to fire nuclear heads towards western territories or airplanes flying over his location. He disobeyed superior orders. He would face a court-martial for treason. However, he is a real hero since he prevented a world war with nuclear destruction. One of the greatest powers was defeated by one man, one of his soldiers.

They miscalculated their actions. They didn't expect other countries to align with their weak rival. The friction between the two sides has spiked to a boiling point. Alexander was told by enemy airplanes to surrender. They wanted him to emerge from his submarine and reach the surface. They didn't know that he was laced with nuclear head torpedoes. He didn't pay attention to the threat. When the biggest warship in the area used its multi-function radar with passive and active sensors, it detected that the submarine was loaded with nuclear bombs and warned the pilots of the airplanes. This first-class destroyer is capable of performing a wide range of operations. However, the presence of this nuke submarine prevented them from acting freely.

The submarine is close to a cluttered sea-land interface. One of the planes dropped a couple of missiles. Thus, they were intercepted by a surgical beam that destroyed them in mid-air. The pilot was reprimanded for shooting at a nuclear-equipped vessel. Thanks to its intervention, there were no major issues. They moved away from the submarine.

A major crisis was averted after the incident, which clearly exposed major flaws on both sides. A geostationary satellite is being used to detect any movement by the adversary.

Nikola was disappointed. All we create with illusion and with our effort is destroyed by wrong ideals on behalf of a group that wants to control the rest of the world. Inventions that were intended for peaceful applications are used for war. Today the boots are marching toward a defenseless country.

If we introspect and look back into our past, any subtle change could have made a difference. We influence the world with our work. If they only knew the magnificence of life, this unique and precious gift, they wouldn't kill one another. It is not in the shallow personality of a brave man who angrily orders the slaughter of millions in order to achieve a goal unknown to his own soldiers. What are we doing here? I don't know. They sent us to protect our country. Protect who from whom?

Those weak people are in terror, and that's because of you and your weapons. They cannot defend against us. Where's the terrible monster we came to fight against? It only exists in the minds of the brainwashers who told us to destroy and kill.

How can we all live in peace? They said, "It comes through enlightenment." It means accepting diversity, including mixed races, and, at the same time, that our differences enrich our world. This is insane. These cavemen are not going to accept the world as it is. They want to mold it it to their liking and benefit. Whose side do you support? I don't stand by any of them. They are all belligerent and obnoxious.

Ignorance is the cause of all evil. Can you imagine our modern world without electricity? No, it is crazy how dependent on electricity we are. It was perplexing how many millions of wires were placed alongside posts, stations, substations, and other equipment. This archaic system provides us with comfort. Every modern device uses some form of electricity. It is either alternating current or direct current. Life would be very different nowadays without electricity. At night, if we could not have the protective electric light in our homes, many things wouldn't be possible. For instance, reading, studying, and entertainment like movie theaters, plays, discos, and bars, among many other activities and businesses. My dream was to have a wireless system that would save all those millions of wires, all that effort, and the issues that are related to that spiderweb in many neighborhoods and cities. However, money imposed its criteria over science.

This electrical system that we use today was built over many decades. Many inventors and great scientists have contributed in one way or another to what we have today. They made great discoveries in the fundamentals and theories of electric and magnetic fields, the conduction of electricity, and the generation of electricity. However, you were the precursor of technological advances that contributed enormously to society. Nobody remembers that, my friend. You developed many electrical devices, most of which never came off the drawing board.

One of Nikola's greatest contributions to modern electrical systems was the development of electrical energy, generated, transmitted, and used in the form of alternating current, or simply AC. The AC system operates at a frequency of 60 Hz, which means that the electrical signal varies in the form of a signal that goes from positive to negative at a rate of 60 times per second. Evidently, this is imperceptible to users, but this parameter is relevant to the company producing the electrical energy. Nikola's unfulfilled dream was to bring wireless electricity to the whole world, which was conceived by Tony and followed by Logan, who ultimately had it in operation on a global scale. This idea consisted of the construction of a huge tower that would generate a large magnetic field surrounding Earth and that, with an antenna, would capture electrical energy to be used in homes and businesses, which, of course, was technologically impossible by that time. Logan took it to the ionosphere as the master had originally planned. We know very well that electrical energy is a big business. The generators serve the energy to the distributors, who carry the electricity through wires to the users. Those are not the most efficient conductors; they are expensive, and they usually have power loss, fires, and many other issues.

Some of Nikola's achievements include the development of an alternating current motor, radar, X-rays, wireless electrical energy transfer, remote control, the electronic microscope, measuring tools, and climate control. He also founded the electrotechnical research laboratory where he discovered the principle of the rotating magnetic field and polyphase alternating current systems. His inventions were relevant to the world. However, they were a century ahead of his era.

Logan was talking to his colleague Dana about the transcendence of Nikola's inventions. Although he faced multiple attacks from the electric power monopolies, this did not stop his enthusiasm and his desire to continue designing and inventing electrical devices that would contribute to the development and welfare of humankind. Nikola was a visionary, worthy of being imitated in many aspects of his life. So was Tony. Dana remarked, "However, I disagree with Logan. Both of your friends were alone." You are right. Nevertheless, it's fair to mention that Tony had his beloved Alina until she died in a confusing incident during a protest against dictatorship in a democracy. That's a valid observation, even though he never got over her. I guess that she was his true love. Do you know the meaning of love? No, not at all. You need to open your mind and look around you. The love of your life could be in front of your eyes.

Nikola's work as an engineer was vital in developing the electrical systems we use today. You are wrong again, Logan. I think you are too naive. What your master created was completely different; a global system. This is pure business nowadays. The two geniuses, Nikola and Tony, were committed to making our lives easier and taking our civilization to the next level in terms of energy. They were both engaged in epic battles with adversaries and governments. Those were diatribes that distracted them from their work.

By that time, Thomas was in favor of direct current (DC), which worked at a power of 100 volts and was difficult to convert to other voltages. On the contrary, Nikola thought that alternating current (AC) was better, as it was easier to carry around. In fact, both currents have their uses; they don't exclude one another.

Dana stated, "Nikola is the scientist who should be famous and who very few people know about." Over a century ago, his extraordinary inventions of electricity caused him such disappointment that he became obsessed with wireless technology, leading him to develop several inventions and theories focused on data transmission. That's what I am currently working on. Trying to develop such primary ideas They are brilliant designs. Guglielmo, his friend and sometimes adversary, had Morse code letters sent across the Atlantic, but Nikola wanted to go further. He wanted to reach for the stars.

Logan starts his speech at the assembly. The magician who humiliated some of his contemporaries with an indiscreet message. The inventor, who went so far as to write that one day it would be possible to transmit telephone signals, documents, music files, and videos around the world using wireless technology. Today, it is possible through wifi. Nikola gave me the toolkit for what I accomplished today. Coming back from not just one portal, but three different portals. One took us straight to the back of the red giant sun. The second one was quite a dreary experience. By accident, we got to a third portal that brought us back to Earth. An unexpected twist of faith from being stranded in interstellar space, far away from home, completely lost in the middle of an unknown galaxy in an alien world, to arriving at the cozy surface of the faithful old Earth.

Even though Nikola himself never achieved such a thing, his prediction came true at the end of the twentieth century, at least commercially, with the popularization of the World Wide Web. Tony continued with his long apology to Nikola. Some delegates are yawning and not really interested in listening to all those compliments. Nevertheless, Logan said, "Cellphones are the result of his futuristic predictions." Before the great depression, he made that bold prediction. Others' responsibility was to develop his idea of a wireless means capable of transmitting images, music, and even video around the world. They completed what he started. Nikola coined the phrase "pocket technology," going so far as to predict the invention of smartphones almost 100 years before they became a reality. We could witness and listen to events as if we were present. He imagined that mobile phones would come to occupy such an important place in our lives that they would be portable and reliable. The very next prediction the master made was drones. At the end of the nineteenth century, he demonstrated a remotely controlled wireless "automaton" device. What today is called a remote-controlled toy boat or a precursor of today's drone. The secretary of the assembly called for a recess to allow delegates and guests to have some snacks and go to the restroom.

Dana encouraged Logan to summarize it. It won't take that long. They are not paying attention to what you're saying. I couldn't care less, my friend. This is for the future generations; they have the right to know what Nikola's legacy is. What Tony did and what we are doing in our current research.

Taking full advantage of wireless communication, robotics, and circuits integrated on a microchip, he amazed his audience with this new technology, and many people thought there was a little monkey controlling the system from inside. Ignorance always plays games with our minds. That's why he was called a magician. Nikola believed that one day, remotely controlled machines would occupy an important place in people's lives. That day has come in our time. He was never far from the truth. He tested all of his experiments by allowing electricity to flow through his body. What's more, he almost lost the fingers on his hand because of the helix of a drone. Today we use drones for packages, transporting food, surveillance, scanning, land surveys, and other uses. The military, on the other hand, took advantage of drones. They use drones for suicidal attacks, transforming the way major powers manage war with robotics.

Most children of the previous century wanted to be pilots or astronauts. They wanted to fly. Nikola was a visionary of high-speed commercial aircraft, with airships capable of circling the globe at high speeds and commercial routes between different countries where there would be capacity for many passengers.

It is still one of his dreams to use wireless energy to propel flying machines without fuel, free from any of the limitations of today's aircraft. His designs using electromagnetism and anti-gravity are the basis for prototypes. We will be able to travel a long distance in less time.

At the time, he said, such a thing might have seemed crazy. However, Nikola was right again. At least as far as speed is concerned. Electric airplanes or spacecraft without fuel, using anti-gravity or electromagnetic force, may sound farfetched. However, we continued his work and accomplished his futuristic dream. We can live the dream today. Even so, we are not ready yet to travel to interstellar space. Our recent adventure just confirmed that there's so much we have to do. We may have spaceships with anti-gravity, but we still have to build more to fit enough people in case we need to massively escape Earth. This is not the right time. We must protect our planet because it's the only one we have.

Now, it is Dana's turn to address the assembly. She starts talking about their trip. Then she shifts to a hot issue, the empowerment of women. Nikola recognized that when a woman is the boss, there may be differences in style, but not in productivity. Women tend to be more detail-oriented and

141

manage resources in a frugal way. Nikola thought highly of women of power. He asserted that women would use wireless technology to gain better education, employment, and ultimately become the dominant sex. As Dana points out, "It is difficult to directly relate technology to the emancipation of women in social and political life." It is clear that we have become world leaders in the technology sector. I traveled with two other scientists to the unknown. I was chosen based on my credentials, not my gender.

Nikola once said, "If its aim is not the improvement of human conditions, science is a perversion." As a woman who feels love and pain and has great emotions, I can tell you that there's no greater sensation than that of an invention. It's like having a baby with your own genes, your blood, and that's something that changes you forever. When ideas turn into something tangible, that can be practical and useful to humankind, that's when everything makes sense. Nikola used to talk about science as the real love of his life. He would forget food, sleep, friends, love, everything when he was at his lab. I've told Logan not to do the same. We all need love, friends, food, and all the things that life brings us.

Nikola was a physicist, mathematician, and philosopher. Any disagreement that arose between Nikola and any other inventor was mostly because of Nikola's brilliance and the others' selfishness. Nikola was hired by businessmen who built their empires in part because of his inventions and discoveries. His legacy is in our hands, and the future is ours.

Logan and Dana hugged and walked away after their presentation at the assembly. It was better than I expected. Yes, it was. As a scientist, the ultimate challenge I can think of is controlling gravity. We have done so thanks to Nikola's ideas. The power is unlimited. It is potentially deadly as a weapon. It is so powerful that it could destroy missiles or remove them from their trajectory. There's a huge military interest in this device. Like everything in life, it depends on how you use it. We have opened leaders' eyes. Now they are in a race to control gravity by using our device. We have sacrificed everything to attempt what was seemingly impossible. We are the only ones who know how to do it. They think that anti-gravity is the key element to interstellar space exploration. It usually pulls us in. What if we could make it push us to propel us into outer space? Nikola used gravity to levitate a plane. We have a gravity-type propulsion system with a vertical launch, so tantalizing, so glittering, to join the race to control gravity to replace fuel and travel farther. The quest for gravity control is turning into madness. You got what they haven't been able to do. You cracked it, Logan. Yes, indeed, with your help, Dana. We beat gravity.

Ian is at the lab, mapping all the portals that they encountered in their recent endeavor into interstellar space. Our government would be really interested in this chart. We won't hide it. It would be useless without a warp-speed spacecraft.

What about the anti-gravity project? That's an official effort to create artificial gravity. Yes, to generate zero gravity and achieve warp speed.

Out of the blue, some scientists announced that by spinning electroconductors at a high speed, they could create a gravitational field. Dana said, "That's ridiculous." They use a vacuum chamber with a disk and rotate it. As soon as the disk reaches a certain velocity, it supposedly exerts a repulsive force on the weight and pushes it up. No, that didn't work out well. They couldn't recreate it in control experiments. Therefore, it doesn't work; it was just a bogus claim made by somebody who wanted to receive some publicity. That was outrageous, a total flop. The media usually jumps to conclusions too early. Yes, and the scientific community is frequently carried along by emotions without conducting additional research to ensure the rigor of its findings. It's vital to go through and make sure that it was not a misleading effect. The anti-gravity project later moved on to a different method using a giant spark plug. Really? Yes, that was a desperate attempt to achieve something to guarantee funds to keep the project in operation. However, gravity was not detected, and the project was canceled. That was an outrageous claim. A total flop.

Prior to their journey, Dana used a quantum gravity gradiometer with a small vacuum chamber. This was at the quantum level. It uses lasers to freeze subparticles, creating a gravitational field caused by the movement of the mass. This unbelievable technology could neutralize the pull of gravity. Are you talking about free falling, Dana? No, nothing to do with it. It's neither the downward swing that momentarily creates this effect of weightlessness nor gravitational traps. Come closer, Logan. What's that? It's a micro-chamber of anti-gravity. Are you kidding me? Not at all. It's real. How do you counter gravity? It's a quantum effect. The quantum world still holds secrets that we must unveil. Logan said, "The electromagnetic quantum vacuum makes obvious the electromagnetic nature of gravity." This quantum cosmic field permeates everything in the cosmos. A magnetic confinement! It's considered wildly unlikely to tame the force of gravity. The conquest of anti-gravity is the aim of scientists and top military leaders. This is an early foray into anti-gravity. This intriguing quantum-verse provides the key elements to accomplish it. We could use it for our spacecraft to travel into interstellar space. Definitely, that's the best option.

Through the eyes of Tesla, I see the future ahead. People may think of electricity when you mention the name Nikola. However, I see a more sustainable world using all possible sources of clean, renewable energy on our planet, the sun, the Milky Way galaxy, the universe, and beyond. It's essential to speed the transition from our less than a planetary civilization to more advanced forms of civilization.

Logan quit science and decided to start his own business, a rocket company for space tourism. He finally married Dana. He lost his sense of appreciation and perspective on life. Logan told Dana that when he was a kid, he hated school. The other kids would follow him home, and they would throw soda cans at his head. They hit me hard. I cried, and I thought that it was insane. However, that's how kids are, especially when you are the most intelligent student in your school and socially awkward. It was clear that others were envious because their minds were just around games and hadn't come up with any brilliant ideas. How were you, Logan? My mind was blowing up with incredible ideas. Nobody seemed to understand that. My parents didn't want me to take the Dumsa test. Which one was that? It was the famous IQ test used to detect prodigies. Why not? They would take me away from the real world to run tests on me eternally. Were you aware that you were different? Not only that, I met Tony, my super star scientist. That was the best moment of my life. How did you cope with your condition? Which one? Do you have more than one? Yes, I do. Asperger's, OCD, and other manias. Don't be silly, handsome. You are cute, Dana!

Now we are geeks. Yeah, right. Why do you like to be alone? I used to enjoy being away from people and their noise. However, I have you now and it is quite different. Why is that? You bring peace and make sense to this lonely life. That's really sweet. We had an excellent rapport back at the lab. Yes, you were my favorite partner.

What did you play as a child? I used to play video games, some sort of addiction. I sought refuge in them. I was submerged for long periods in that surreal world. I imagine that it was your escape from this dumb world. You are right again. How many children would you like to have, Logan? I don't know. I think that's up to you. No, we have to agree on how many. I want four. What about you, Logan? I would like as many as possible. Are you crazy? Yes, I'm crazy about you. What about six, Dana? We can give it a try. Don't worry about money; we'll have enough to support them. Maybe we can adopt some. I don't know if I can deal with that. Come on, Logan!

How are we going to run this start-up? I have some money I got when I sold my first company. When was that? When I was sixteen, I had a computer coding business that I sold for a few bucks.

Dana had a miscarriage. She's at the hospital. Logan runs to get to her. My sweetheart, I'm so sorry. Nobody is really prepared for this. You prefer to be buried before your children. That's the worst loss. It is really painful. Don't worry, Logan. I'm pretty sure we're going to have many children. Whatever you say, dear Dana. Her therapist tells Logan, "Even though Dana is devastated after her loss, she pretends that it didn't affect her much. However, she is crying inside."

This was a turning point for the Dana. From then on, she started to attend a temple to pray, and she got closer to spirituality. Where are you going, Dana? I'm going to the temple. What for? I need to pray. It usually clears my mind. Didn't you go yesterday and the day before yesterday? Yes, I did. Do you have any problem with that? No, not at all. Tell me the truth. I think you are dedicating too much time to it. Join me! Not today. I promise you that I will go with you next time. That's a deal, handsome.

I've found a place here among the lost souls. A priest approaches her. You are not a lost soul anymore. You've found your core! Yes, I did. Thanks for reminding me. That's what we are here for. Are you ready for the ultimate ritual? No, I think you are never ready for this. What's going to happen? We are going to get rid of our attachments in life, destroy the past and become clean souls. How do you attain such things? We are going to burn the temple. Are you kidding me? No, this is serious. Take some logs, matches, or whatever you see in the courtyard. The group is gathering. We are going to start in a few minutes. What else should I do? Write your most painful memories on a piece of paper, get a lace and attach it to one log. What for? It will burn and your pain will fade away with the fire. The flames will purify your soul and eliminate any blocks in your chakras. Dana did as he instructed her. Although she got teary eyes, she continued, gasping and weeping. The bell sound was heard all over the temple. The ceremony is about to start. The line was long; people humming and chanting a mantra were walking toward a fire. It's comforting. Dana started crying and laughing at the same time. They moved a few meters away. However, they still felt the heat from there. Dana shouted, "Thank you." A relief that signified getting rid of the burden of her previous loss.

Logan keeps up with the creation of the new company. This is like having a baby. A lot of preparation. I need to prepare people for space tourism. A marketing campaign would help us attract the attention of the right people who can afford a high-priced ticket. Space is going to be the new frontier for tourism.

Dana told Logan that she was pregnant again. I'm really happy. Let's celebrate it. We have to celebrate it twice. Really? Yes, handsome. We are doubly lucky. You have been through a period of crisis. You deserve this. What's that? We're going to a restaurant in Paris. We're using one of our fastest airplanes. We'll get there in two hours.

I look forward to seeing our spacecraft arrive at other planets. It is a dream of mine to start space mining. Diamonds, hydrocarbons, and many other unknown minerals are offered by Titan, Neptune, and many other celestial bodies. We may find other civilizations out there.

Why did you tell me, "Darkness doesn't mean evil"? You know, dear Dana, that it can refer to anything that has never been exposed to light. Lightlessness? Yes, light beyond boundaries.

Dana is talking to her best friend Lisa. After six children and twenty years of marriage, Dana and Logan got divorced. Logan has been obsessed with his work and I have been too busy with the children, even though I have some babysitters and people who help me with the housework, it is strenuous, it drains my energy and I had enough. When I was at home, his mind was elsewhere. We seldom talk about science like we used to do. He made me feel insignificant and useless. It made me think of how our dynamic or lack of interaction would have affected our six children. Counseling has been a source of hope. However, he is running two companies, and he didn't dedicate time to putting into action the piece of advice our therapist recommended. After a month and a few therapy sessions, he gave me an ultimatum. How did he dare to do that to you, the mother of his children? He was cold-hearted. What did he want you to do? He said, "We either fix this marriage today or get

149

divorced tomorrow." What did you do? I did nothing. I thought that he was just stressed. I wanted to give it a try for our children and for ourselves. We deserved a second chance. Nevertheless, he filed for divorce the next morning. He felt numb and strangely relieved. It seemed that it was what he wanted. Why do you say that? Six weeks later, he proposed to Briana, an actress. That bastard! Things developed very quickly. What are you going to do, Dana? I am open to any possibility. I would say yes to any man who seemed half sensible. Don't do that, my friend. That's a recipe for disaster. I know that you don't want to be alone. Listen, do you think that there's any man who wants to be with a mother and six children? There will surely be somebody with an open heart. Besides money seekers, I don't see anybody else. My parents are traumatized by this unexpected outcome. What are you going to do with your life? I need to pick up the pieces and go on with my life, for the kids and for myself. I owe that to them. I will take a trip to Europe. Not for vacation; it would be more of a distraction. I need to get away from him and that opportunistic lady. I don't want to see him again. That's not possible, my friend. You share custody of the children, and he has the right to see them. Yes, that's true. However, he doesn't have to see me.

Logan and his beloved actress didn't last very long. It was just passion overboard that lasted for three years. It all ended with a divorce. She broke up with him. She couldn't stand his behavior and the way he treated her. After a severe emotional shock for a couple of weeks, it was hard for him to even meet people. He was visibly sad in public. Logan choked on his broken heart, working for too many hours nonstop. He shouldn't have done that. It was so painful that it hurt his brain.

Logan was thinking, that hen more trouble came over. I got involved with Britt, who was getting divorced from her famous husband, a renowned actor. I have to do something to protect Britt. Logan said, "That man is crazy." Jealousy pushed him into domestic violence. There's no reason to do that. They split and are getting a divorce. Why the drama? We are all adults; thus, we understand how life is. When you break up, a new love takes over with no grief for broken hearts. I will provide her with surveillance and 24/7 security. She got a restraining order against her husband.

Nobody is worried. Tony and Nikola see that Logan is acting so erratic, unstable, reckless, doing things mechanically and acting impulsively. His OCD is out of control. His personal life is wrecked by his jumping from one relationship to another. I heard he's also suffering from repetition compulsion. He's subconsciously driven to recreate certain familiar situations or relationships from the past in an attempt to resolve them. He lacks a singular explanation for his behavior. He goes untreated since he denies his problem and won't accept it. The need to get it right gravitates towards him and pushes Logan to get involved in relationships and circumstances that mimic the ones where he didn't feel accepted or loved.

Logan knows he's self-destructive, harms others, and undergoes a re-victimization process. My connection with Tony and Nikola was lost. How did

I get here? I guess I should wait before jumping into another relationship. I met the wrestler, then that gorgeous model, later the news anchor, and so on. I have to take some time off, some sort of love vacation, no more love in desperation. I haven't figured out why my previous relationships haven't worked in the long run. My condition makes me get obsessed with relationships. I'm all in or nothing at all. My therapist tells me that my codependence is killing me. What about loneliness? Sleeping alone is unacceptable. She said, "I'm afraid of abandonment." I may still be the same kid that was bullied at school, crying alone in the darkness. Every ailment brings out the best in me for creation.

I have to accept that there's power in accepting your darkness and fighting your demons. I won't be crushed by my inner fight. Redirect my energies to more productive endeavors; I will return to science. Get a new life, a new identity. Don't dismay Logan. We are still with you. Where have you been all this time? We have been watching you destroy yourself. Why didn't you do something? We cannot fight your own battles. You need to defeat all the darkness you have inside.

I will honor my mentors. It's time for me to create electric vehicles. I will name them after Tony and Nikola. I believe space tourism will catch on in the near future. Meanwhile, I am going to have a space cargo business. I will deliver satellites for governments. This is the beginning of the privatization of space.

Logan is talking to his mother, Thea, a psychologist who believes in raising children with love and care and not physical punishment. His father, Luke, is a doctor, a surgeon to be more specific. Thea patronizes Logan. She's always been overprotective of her children. As they talked, they remembered their ordeal coping with Luke's abusive behavior. She would pay the toll whenever she confronted him about their children's punishment. As soon as she got divorced, she stopped falling in the shower or having bruises. I know, Mom, that he did all those awful things to you. He was not a friendly man to be around with. He has mood swings and uncontrollable anger outbursts.

Logan never talks about his father. He had been sent away since he was little. He spent a whole lot of time in boarding schools. Later, he was accepted by Tony to join his scientific team, and he was also teaching at an Ivy League university. That was his way out of living hell. I can tell you that my childhood, between bullies at school and my father's unpredictable behavior, made my childhood sorrowful. I could cope with my life back then just by playing video games and creating computer coding. I created my own tiny world. I got obsessed with learning and mastering a whole new skillset as a means of escaping reality. This body of knowledge replaced my lack of social skills.

My father was a luddite. Did that affect you? I think that to some extent, since he didn't like machines or technology, and that was a disadvantage I had compared to other children. Furthermore, he refused to buy me a computer. He said that computers would never do anything. How wrong he was! Although that was a punch in the gut, I desperately wanted to learn, and this was a limitation that wouldn't stop me. I know that you wanted to be an astronaut. Yes, they were my heroes. It was foreseeable that you would get involved in space exploration somehow.

I want to build a base on Mars. Nikola and Tony will help me get there. You have the knowledge and the resources to get to Mars. Although you need more people involved in that ambitious dream, you have an extraordinary ally. Who's that? You forgot about our friend Barlow. You are right. I completely forgot about him. You need to focus on your priorities. Besides my business, that's my priority. I would say that it is over anything in my life. Even your family? Why didn't you answer, Logan? You kept me thinking about my purpose in life and my family as part of a bigger picture.

What about the novelist? Dana? Yes, your ex-wife. We are divorced now. You have six children. Yes, we do. I wish I could see them more often. Why don't you do that? I am afraid that I am not a good father. I was never prepared to become a father. Are you ever ready for the challenges that life brings you? No, not really. Don't look for excuses; claim back your fatherhood, and do it better than your father did. I'll try my best. No, don't do that. Your best effort is not enough for your children, Logan. I understand. Thanks for the advice. Nikola told Logan, "From now on, you are going to see through my eyes." What does that mean? You are going to have my vision, my acumen, and all my expertise. Does that include a connection between our consciousnesses? Yes, it

154

does. And as a bonus, you will be linked to Tony, too. That's fantastic!

This last conversation brought back some painful early memories. I have to deal with them. It's true, my children need me in the present. He went to visit his children and decided to spend the whole weekend with them. This is a beginning. Logan told his children, "Some of you are adolescents, others are still young. No matter how old you are, you will always be in my heart. I won't let you alone any longer." He hugged all of them. This reconciliation brings hope to a broken relationship with his descendants.

Logan is preparing the team for a base on Mars and a future human settlement on the red planet. We have chosen the area for the base. Where's that? It's a crater in the rocky desert of the red planet, with hues of orange and brown. An orange tone on the horizon covers the landscape of the terrain. We still have to deal with weightlessness and cold temperatures. On Mars, the average temperature is minus 60 °C and the atmosphere is unbreathable." Who is overseeing the mission? Barlow will help us with that part and also with his expertise.

For months, the team will be isolated in space under a dome. There are many conditions required for humans on long missions in space. The flight has begun. Logan, Ian, Destinee, and Ryan are the human members of the mission, alongside three cutting-edge robots. Now there's no turning back. Upon arrival, they will be ready to deploy the station. This "Martian station" is going to be assembled in a couple of days with the help of robotics. Meanwhile, we'll have to live in the spacecraft. We will only be able to leave the station in a special suit to explore the red planet. "It's a dream come true," says Logan. I know Nikola's eyes are on us. "It's something we've been working on for several years. I'm very happy to be here.

For the station's inauguration tomorrow, Logan and Ian are getting everything ready. Our silver outfit weighs about 50 kilos and takes two or three hours to put on. We have to develop a lighter one while we are here.

Teamwork as well as coherence are essential for the success of this mission. We will acquire new abilities by working together. "It's like a marriage, only in a marriage one can leave, and on Mars you can't," Logan comments wryly. All members of "the crew" were volunteers and had passed many physical and psychological tests in order to participate in the mission. Logan reckons with Barlow. Our underground base is not far from here. As soon as you have settled all your stuff, I will give you a tour of our facilities.

Destinee's father used to take her to the space museum when she was little. She collected airplanes, and when she heard that Logan was looking for astronauts, she said to herself that she had to apply. She's the only woman in the team.

They partnered with specialists on Earth for the research of the station. They built this solar-powered, polygon-shaped base. Now, they are moving the parts to assemble the whole structure on Mars. Tomorrow it will be ready for us. The inside will provide us comfort with a small kitchen and bunk beds since most of the space is for

156

scientific experiments, and their results could be crucial for future colonization of the planet.

Everything is ready for the inauguration of the station. They started the live transmission to Earth. Astronauts greet their families with a special message. After the ceremony, they will have to test a prototype drone and autonomous robotic vehicles powered by wind and solar energy to map the territory. Ryan is a microbiologist. He will be in charge of assessing the potential for microbial contamination, for instance, the risk of introducing terrestrial bacteria to Mars that could wipe out any existing life on the red planet. "It would be a big problem," he says, pointing to what is considered one of the biggest challenges in the conquest of space. He will accompany Barlow to look closer at life on the planet.

In addition to testing equipment and technologies, the mission also wants to study human behaviors under the conditions of the red planet. Search for water and areas that are suitable for human settlements. Barlow guides Logan and the team to the underground base his race constructed on Mars. How many aliens are there in your base? We are a group of twelve. Just twelve? Yes, our civilization is not like yours. We are not too many. Our population is less than one hundred thousand living entities. Why entities? Aren't you the same? No, not at all. We are a diverse society. We have rescued beings from other worlds and they have been inserted into our world. Through the gate, they entered the underground habitat. Sobac came to welcome them. "You must be Logan." How do you know? Barlow has sent us your profiles in advance. We were expecting all of you. Do you sometimes go to the surface of the planet? We usually fly over. We seldom walk on the surface. Do you think that we can settle on the surface? Barlow interrupted. It's up to you and the technology that you are going to use to build your station and future domes. My recommendation is that you start your station on the ground with a first settlement underground. Is there any running water on the planet? There certainly is water. However, it is not liquid. It is in a solid state, basically frozen into ice in the poles and other areas of the planet. We'll use some to extract hydrogen as a fuel for our vehicles. You can also get hold of eolic energy.

The colonization of Mars will not be easy. There will be accidents. Many colonists would die. And it is possible that the first settlements will end tragically. It is highly likely that the plans will have to be modified to adapt to the terrain and the conditions of the environment. Logan is optimistic that they will comply with the chronology for human settlements on Mars. The whole process will be accomplished within ten years after this mission. The epic evacuation could begin with the first trip landing in a year or so. If we successfully complete the stages we have planned, the start of colonization will not be a round trip in the style of manned-moon missions. Instead, it will be just a one-way ticket with lots of robots and machinery at first, followed by a one-year stay of the team until the first massive arrival of immigrants. It's a fascinating vision that runs from the first launch of five unmanned rovers to the red planet to this first manned mission to Mars that we lead today.

The timeline is anchored in our current scientific knowledge, various action plans, and a basic idea for the future of humanity: to survive as a species in the long-term. We must save the Earth, and it is imperative that we settle on other planets. Logan's plan of endeavoring throughout the universe is nothing new. It's Nikola's dream come true. After getting onto Martian soil, they come with the determination of founding the first Martian city. The knowledge acquired in these explorations with Barlow is vital for future crews coming to the red planet. How are we going to materialize this dream? We have everything written in detail. Thus, there's little room for improvisation. Nikola says, "From satellites, to quantum batteries, to solar panels to create and connect underground colonies, all are pieces of a master plan for the colonization of the red planet." Yes, Nikola's guidance is paramount to attaining our goals.

The odyssey begins with the arrival on Mars of ten starships full of cargo and robots. Are there replacements? Yes, the new crew will take over for another year. We will be back at the end of their service. Some of these starships do not carry humans. I know that. They have the vital machinery and systems to establish the first base on Mount Erebus, as well as basic resources such as oxygen, water, dehydrated food, and medical supplies. From solar panels to cover an area of ten soccer fields, to fuel, spacesuits, inflatable habitats, systems for recycling waste, and a constellation of four satellites for communication between the future inhabitants of the first base, an orbital wireless Internet network.

The spaceships also carry rovers and robotic animals, which will be in charge of installing all these components as well as cleaning the terrain while awaiting the arrival of more humans.

As a result of progress, the next Earth-to-Mars approach window will bring 30 starships loaded to the hilt with vital supplies and with ten thousand humans to permanently inhabit the underground city. The scientific team will be replaced by a bigger crew led by Logan. His return has been long awaited. He will arrive accompanied by scientists, engineers, doctors, and military scientists who will stay on Mars after acclimating to Martian gravity after months of space travel. They will have many missions to complete as they battle the harsh surface conditions. Researching the terrain, unpacking equipment, and securing the base while living in their ground station will only be part of their work. The key will be to start up the first fuel factory that will be used to travel back and forth to Earth. Logan will also begin projects such as the first self-replicating and self-repairing robots, some sort of advanced 3D printer technology, the cultivation of plants genetically modified to grow in Martian soil, and the use of cyanobacteria to generate fertilizers from the nitrogen in the Martian atmosphere. Terraforming Mars is a long-term goal.

The beginning of agriculture on a large scale and the visit of the first space tourists to Mars will happen in a few months when the next stage brings a large fleet. These are people who would pay up to $50 million to take the ride and work like the rest of the colonists. They may end up being permanent residents of the red planet. Among this group of humans, there will be the first team of farmers: botanists whose mission will be to set up the first greenhouse system to produce the first crops to feed the colonists. It is during this period that the first Martian fruit and the first Martian meal will be available. Food production will be essential to reduce the volume of goods shipped from Earth and, later, to achieve total independence from Earth.

In this phase, the first factory and the first permanent fuel depot will also be commissioned. And the first architects on the planet will use robots and 3D printing technology that blends Martian soil and a polymer from plants grown on the planet to construct buildings and other structures. Inside these domes and the underground cities, colonists will place habitats connected to interior modules taken from the spaceships themselves until they are autonomous in terms of energy, which means they can gain sustainability in a few weeks from the landing.

On the brink of food independence, at this new stage, most of the food is already produced on Martian soil thanks to advanced gardening techniques. The population will grow exponentially, with the arrival of 200 spaceships loaded with colonists and the return of previous scientists assigned to the station. They will begin to survey the terrain to build the first ground means of transportation.

The next year, the first animals arrive in cargo spaceships from other Earth nations. More people will join the colony, increasing the population to almost half a million people. The first marine creatures will also arrive, which will serve as the basis for the creation of the first self-sustaining habitat using excess water that cannot be consumed by humans, a by-product of fuel creation.

Barlow is very cautious at this time, and he added, "Your ultra-optimistic view does not include the losses we have had already." It is sad that this year we had the first funeral on Mars. In reality, quite a few more people have died due to accidents or natural causes. Humans are too fragile for the hostile environment of this planet.

Nikola warned Logan, "Many of the people coming to the colony are not bringing any knowledge or contributing to its progress." What should I do? I must urge the government to impose a more strict selection of those coming as residents. We have the right to return to Earth those who do not meet our standards of a typical Martian citizen. Now, it is commonplace to have arrivals and departures on a weekly basis. The spaceships arrive as small flotillas when Earth and Mars are closer than in previous years, with a shorter travel time than usual.

The construction of the first hospital will begin in a month, and people will decide to stay here forever. The first big wave of migrants will arrive at the end of the year. One million people will arrive with the intention of staying permanently and making their lives on Mars. With a population of almost two million people, there is no stopping them. The first marriage and the first Martian television program have taken place. Some things do not change, not even in the future, or at least not in the short-run.

Ian and Destinee recently discovered the first large caves, which are fundamental for the creation of large-scale cities protected from radiation.The network of tunnels that will connect different points on the planet is in the making. The rest of the nations on the planet will build their own habitats beyond our station. Alpha, Beta, Delta, and other bases will also be the first manifestation of Martian architecture and a new humanity.

The birth of babies, whether genetically manipulated or not, will be the fundamental key to the ultimate fate of Mars and the humans settled there. Not because it marks the beginning of the reproduction of all species on the planet, but because of something much more profound.

Nikola is telepathically reaching all of the people in the colonies through Logan and the communication systems. He tells them, "On a technological level, the chronology of the next 5 years is an evolutionary path with new cities that will continue to grow, new machines, and new infrastructures. Cherish your future."

Soon, with the first natives, will come the first sense of identity. Humans will begin to stop being terrestrial and become Martians. They will have a different culture, a product of seeing life with completely different parameters based on a sense of belonging to the red planet.

Everything on Mars, from the landscape, the climate, the daily struggle, the value of things in the face of the harshness of the environment, the feeling of permanent risk, and even the completely different vision of sunrises and sunsets, will transform the human beings settled there. The whole Martian life experience will be different from the terrestrial experience. It stands to reason that everything that makes us human, from music to relationships, will also be different from the terrestrial.

Along with this new Martian identity will come a new society and total independence from Earth. They will be our beloved brothers on another planet. This won't be anything new for future generations. It has already happened hundreds of times in the universe, in other galaxies, and on different planets. We will have to wait to see if the Martians take into account the mistakes of their Earthling ancestors and decide to build a fairer society and a better planet.

About the Author

Fernando Fernandez Solano is a Dominican Republic native who resides in Santo Domingo. Fernando is the writer of the book series trilogy "Number 2"

Vol. I "Death and Space-time".
Vol. II "A Quantum Leap: Escaping From Heaven".
Vol. III: "Artificial Intelligence: Beyond Boundaries."

"His Metaverse" is his latest book.

All of them are available in Spanish too, and in the following formats: e-book, paperback, and hardcover.
Furthermore, writing became his passion to express himself, mainly through writing poetry and taking a stand on social issues. When not writing, Fernando loves traveling, hiking, nature, and the outdoors. He enjoys watching pro sports, as well as listening to music and playing games online.